MW00890062

A Wish for
Pegeen

A Peggy Tregarth Adventure

Lucille Callard

LCCN: 2009905797
ISBN: 1-4392-4476-6

Cover design: Peter Solomon

Acknowledgements

My thanks and appreciation to David Chapple, a Cornish fisherman, and to his wife, Jacqueline Chapple, who grew daffodils and violets for the London markets. Their help was invaluable in writing this book

Many thanks again to my patient editors, Nicole Hill, Ed.M and Loraine Volz, MSW

Dedication

For my grandchildren, Matt Hill and Jacqui Hill,
and for Lyn Peterson - my first fan.

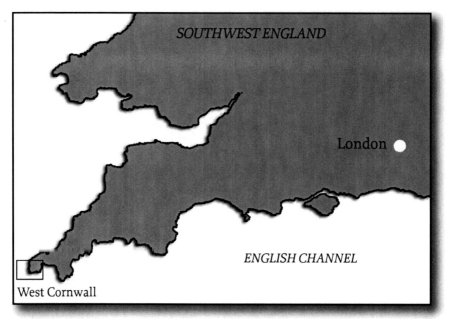

SOUTHWEST ENGLAND

London

ENGLISH CHANNEL

West Cornwall

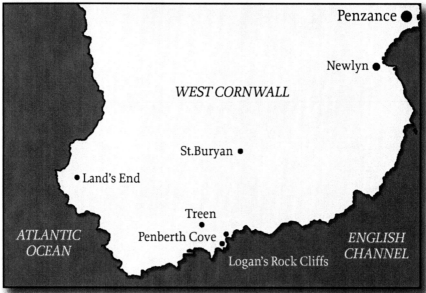

Penzance

Newlyn

WEST CORNWALL

St.Buryan

Land's End

Treen

ATLANTIC
OCEAN

Penberth Cove

Logan's Rock Cliffs

ENGLISH
CHANNEL

Author's Note:

Cornwall, the historic homeland of the Cornish people, is a county in the southwest of England, on the peninsula that lies to the west of the River Tamar and Devon. It is considered to be one of the six historic Celtic nations by many scholars. Cornwall is filled with myths, legends, and folklore. Many seek the magic to be found there. *A Wish for Pegeen* is set in Cornwall. Although the towns, villages, cliffs, and coves you will read about are real, all the people named are fictitious as are the school and church mentioned in the book. The fishing crisis, which put half of the Cornish fishermen out of work, and the conservation issues addressed in the novel, is based on fact.

CONTENTS

Chapter One

Spring Break

Peggy Tregarth sat restlessly on the green vinyl bench seat of the bus as it made its way slowly through the narrow streets. She looked through her brown and cream backpack for something to eat. Sighing, she gave up and gazed out of the window. The ocean was peaceful today, gently lapping the pebbled shore, deceptive in its tranquility. It's like a wild stallion grazing, Peggy decided. Like Tor would be.

"Newlyn," the driver announced cheerfully.

Peggy glanced up to see if anyone she knew was getting on the bus. Her eyes widened. She stared at the lanky, teenage boy who jumped the steps. The boy had bright green hair. She couldn't help staring. His hair was not only bright green, it also looked like a bush in a windstorm. His jeans were full of rips and tears and his black tee was decorated with a bright red electric guitar. Why would anyone want to look like that? Peggy shook her head, and was about to dismiss him, when she smelled something bad. The boy had brought it on the bus with him. No, she was wrong about that, she realized immediately. The boy himself was the bad smell. He smelled like vomit. Peggy wrinkled her nose in disgust. She tensed as he hesitated beside her bench, and then chose to sit in front of her. She tried holding her breath, but the moment she had to take air, she felt sick. She would have to move and now!

Peggy turned to see where the empty seats were. Jimmy Wallace and Dave Turner were two rows behind her. Dave Turner was really overweight, with dark hair and brown eyes. Jimmy Wallace was an athlete, with blond curly hair and blue eyes. Jimmy was bending over, his finger in his mouth, making retching noises. Dave was snorting with laughter. Peggy couldn't resist grinning. There was an empty row in front of them, but she didn't want to move there. It was weird, really. Before she had noticed how special Jimmy Wallace was, she sat in front of them, or behind them. It hadn't mattered where they sat, or where she sat, but now, the more she liked Jimmy, the more she tried to avoid him. In fact, every time Jimmy looked right at her, she felt her face go red.

The bus lurched as the driver shifted down for the long climb up Paul Hill. The smell of fish was strong today. No matter how many times they hosed down Newlyn Fish Market after the busy morning's trading, the fishy smell stayed in the air, a part of the buildings, the pilings, and pavements there. Normally Peggy didn't mind the smell of fish. She had grown up with it, but mixed with the smell of Gross Green right in front of her, she decided that in future, she should always carry nose plugs.

There were only three empty seats on the bus – two in front of Jimmy and Dave and the other beside Gross Green. Peggy groaned inwardly and leaned back in her seat as far as she could. It didn't help. Gross Green was now crunching and smacking as he pushed handfuls of crisps into his mouth.

Peggy rolled her eyes. She should think of something else, she decided, and if that didn't work, she would have to stop the bus and walk home! Her mother had told her that if she was forced into an unpleasant situation, she should try to think of something she liked to make things better. Of course, her mother had said that when she went on a field trip with the school to an art museum and had been grouped with two girls that she absolutely hated. It had kind of worked so she tried it again when similar situations came up, but she had never been confronted with vomit smells before. Still, she could give it a try.

What should she think about? Her favorite thing in the whole world was *The Sunrise*. She imagined herself out in her father's boat, the tiller under her hand, holding her steady while her father pulled the lobster and crab pots. She absolutely loved going to sea. Maybe her father would let her take the boat out by herself soon. Okay, the currents were strong in Penberth cove, the rocks dangerous, but that's what made it exciting. She definitely needed more practice, though. Her father was always at sea, but he didn't let her come with him often, even when she was home, with nothing to do, begging him to take her. Sometimes he didn't say she couldn't come, but looked at her mother and her mother always shook her head. Peggy sighed. It was probably because her mother needed her help in the daffodil fields.

"St Buryan," the bus driver said.

Gross Green got up, crumbled his crisp packet, and tossed it on the floor. Peggy watched him leave with relief, but the air that came into the bus when the door opened blasted his vomit smell right back at her. Peggy held her breath until she was gasping for air. As the bus moved on, Peggy looked out of the window. Gross Green was staring at her. He raised his hand and bowed low.

"Do you know him?" Jill Willis said, as she slipped into

the seat next to Peggy.

"What?" Peggy gasped, glad to be breathing again.

"Michael Barrett," Jill answered. "Can you believe what he did to his hair? His mum is a friend of my mum's, and she said he dyed his hair because he's going to be famous."

"For having green hair and smelling like vomit?" Peggy asked, in disbelief.

"No, silly, he plays guitar in a band."

"Whatever," Peggy said, losing interest in Gross Green. "St Buryan gets out today, right?"

Jill nodded. She was a pretty girl, as tall as Peggy, with blond hair down to her shoulders and dark brown eyes. Her face was flushed with excitement. "Can you believe it? No school for three weeks!"

Peggy grinned, "I was just sitting here planning my holiday. What are you doing?"

"I'm going to stay with my Aunt Jessie for a week. She lives in Hull. I can't wait! She said she would give me a manicure and a pedicure. That's what she does for a living. She works in a real hairdressers. I've been trying to decide what color I should choose. Blue would look interesting, but what if I was wearing something that clashed with blue? And if I wore blue lipstick to match, I would look weird, don't you think? I was also thinking about magenta, but that could clash, too."

Peggy tried to picture her fingernails and her toe nails painted bright blue. Her mother would throw a fit – a foam at the mouth fit. Jill was lucky to have a mother that would let her paint her nails and stuff. Her mother wouldn't even let her paint her nails a pale pink. "You could try one hand in blue and the other in magenta, then you could decide what you liked best."

Jill smiled. "Good idea. I think Aunt Jessie would let me experiment. She's really nice. Are you going away, Peggy?"

"No, I'm going to work on taking my dad's boat out on my own. I have ..."

"Sparnan," the bus driver announced.

"Maybe you could come over and we could do something? I don't leave for Hull until the week after next," Jill said as she hurried off the bus. At Peggy's window, Jill raised her hand to her ear, her pinky and thumb extended. Peggy nodded. Maybe she would call Jill. She was only eleven, over a year younger than her, but next year she would be going to her school, *Trinity*. They could sit together and she would be protected forever from Gross Green!

Peggy heard Jimmy laughing about something. He was always laughing. Peggy liked that. She liked it a lot. Peggy didn't find most things funny. She always laughed with joy, though, when she was out in *The Sunrise*. She thought about what she had told Jill. She knew it wouldn't really happen. Mum would make her spend most of her school holiday working with the daffodils: picking, bunching, and packing them in shipping boxes for the London flower markets. She had to make a plan and think of some creative excuses to get out of helping her mother. Even if she couldn't go out in the boat, there were so many other things she wanted to do that had nothing to do with mud, weeds, and daffodils!

As Peggy considered her options, still hearing Jimmy's laughter, she had no idea that she would be making a totally different plan before the weekend was over – a plan to try to stop her world from crashing down around her, and Jimmy Wallace would not only help her with her plan, he would really and truly save her life.

"Treen," the driver announced.

Peggy grabbed her backpack and jumped off the bus. She hurried down the hill towards home. She heard the boys laughing again and glanced back up the hill. Jimmy and Dave were still standing at the top, looking right at her. Peggy flushed with embarrassment and hurried on. They were probably laughing at her because Gross Green had bowed to her. Did they think she was a friend of his or something?

There were four houses in the valley, two on the right of the road, two on the left. Peggy turned right onto the stony lane leading to her house, Chyoak Cottage, relieved that Jimmy and Dave could no longer see her.

Nimbob, her brown and black tabby cat, was curled up on the window seat, basking in the late afternoon sun. He yawned, stretched, and jumped off the seat to greet her. Peggy grabbed him and hugged him. "You're the best cat in the whole world," she said affectionately. Nimbob purred his agreement.

There was note on the kitchen table, printed in her mother's distinctive hand. Peggy read it aloud. "Working in the daffodil fields. I need your help."

"Daffodils? I only just broke up from school, Mum!" She folded the sides of the note to make a paper plane and sailed it across the kitchen. Nimbob pounced on it and batted it across the floor.

Peggy ran upstairs to her bedroom. She dropped her backpack onto the floor and pulled off her yellow and brown striped tie. She hated tying that tie. Now she wouldn't have to tie it for three whole weeks! She tossed her tan school uniform on the bed, and slipped on her old jeans and yellow jumper. Her pigtails were next. She ran into the bathroom and pulled off the rubber bands. "No more pigtails for three weeks, either!" she cried happily, running a brush through her brown curly hair.

Peggy rode the stair banister back down to the kitchen, and hurried into the scullery. The larder was sparsely filled. The oven and stove were cold. "Mum never bakes any more," she grumbled to herself. Settling for an apple, Peggy blew a kiss to Nimbob and ran outside, slamming the door behind her.

As she turned to go down the path, she heard a weird clunking noise. She was totally unaware that it was a sound that she would soon hear in her mind over and over again - a sound that would give her nightmares that very night. She reached for the doorknob to go back in, to see what it was that had made that sound, but decided not to bother. She would see what it was when she got back.

Chapter Two

Mystical Piskies

Peggy ducked under the clotheslines across the stone pathway. The two white plastic lines were filled with white towels, sheets, and her father's blue work shirts, pinned to the lines with wooden pegs. Her mother had a washing machine, but she always preferred to hang the clothes outside to dry in the wind and the sun. It was Peggy's job to fold the wash, and to bring it in, but she decided to do that later. She paused at the end of the path. If she turned right, the path led to the daffodil fields where her mother was working. If she turned left, she would be in the heifer field, a shortcut to the cliffs. Of course, if she went around to the back of the cottage, she could just take a quick look at the fox, penned up in the chicken coop. What harm would that do? Granny's orders about the fox were firm, though. She had to wait until after six tonight before she could go near him. Everybody was convinced that the fox had rabies, or was sick.

Peggy ran along the path to the field where the young brown and white cows were grazing. She climbed over the gate, crossed the field, and jumped over the stone stile steps. The crisp breeze, moist and salty, cooled her as she ran. There was a road and more fields to cross, but it was not long before Peggy was in her favorite place – the Logan Rock cliffs.

How brilliant her cliffs looked today, strong craggy fortresses the stormy seas could only rage against. Seagulls wheeled above her in the blue sky. "If only I could open my arms wide and fly with you," Peggy cried enviously. She watched them for a while, and decided that the next best thing to flying would to be on Tor's back. Like the wind itself, they would race through the heather. But Tor was only her fantasy horse. He was almost real because she wanted him so much.

Peggy looked carefully about her. The cliffs stretched on either side of her for miles. There was no one in sight. Although she had not played her once favorite game for a very long time, it was the only thing she wanted to do today. Grinning, she pretended to mount Tor. Pawing the ground, snorting, rearing, Peggy galloped across the cliff top towards Logan Rock.

"You're a fine horse, Peggy Tregarth."

Peggy stopped abruptly. Her pink cheeks darkened as she looked sheepishly at the old woman who had stepped out from behind the huge granite rock. "I ... I was just so happy, Granny. We broke up from school today." She looked around to see if anyone else had seen her. "I guess I looked really stupid."

Granny Poldune grunted. "And what's stupid about riding such a fine horse? It's a grand thing to do in my opinion." Peggy felt a rush of warmth for the old woman. Granny had a canny knack of understanding everything.

"It was here that I saw them that night, Peggy." Granny stepped back to the side of the rock, and peered into the crevices. "Oh, they'll have none of me today. Not that I've not always felt them when they're about, but I've not seen them since that night."

Peggy stood beside the old woman. All she could see was the granite rock, sparkling in the sunshine, gull droppings, and a large black ant climbing laboriously up one side. "Who did you see, Granny?" she asked curiously.

Granny Poldune gathered the long, gray skirt of her dress and sat on a low granite ledge. "There's room," she said. Peggy sat beside her and waited patiently for Granny to tell her story. She had learned as a small child that Granny would tell her things in her own way and in her own time.

Granny Poldune closed her eyes and rocked her body slowly in time with the wind soughing in the heather. While she waited, Peggy studied Granny's sandy brown, soft skin face. There were hundreds of tiny lines running across each other all over her cheeks, especially around her eyes and mouth.

"It was a warm summer's night with a full moon shining over the whole of Cornwall," Granny began in her special remembering voice. "Grandfather was fierce about the nights when the moon lit up the beaches and coves like it was day. His work was dangerous enough."

A small brown rabbit hopped between Granny's black, dusty, high-buttoned boots, and snuggled down. Peggy leaned over to stroke it, but Granny's gnarled, bony hand was quick to stop her. "He came to me for a rest, child. Leave him be."

Peggy nodded and withdrew her hand. Wild animals trust Granny just like I do, she thought. She looked at the old woman, expecting her to go on with her story, but Granny was gazing into the past, smiling at a memory of an event long gone.

"Is this the grandfather who was a pirate or a smuggler

or something, Granny?" asked Peggy, who had heard gossip about Granny Poldune's grandfather for years.

"I suppose some might have called him that," Granny said. "No braver man than he ever sailed the Cornish seas." She pursed her thin lips, and nodded in agreement with herself. "Now, at the time I was telling you about, I was just a slip of a girl, but it was me who was to signal my grandfather ashore that night. I was proud he trusted me like he did, but for all of that, I almost failed him."

Peggy hid her smile behind her hand. It was hard to imagine that Granny Poldune was ever a 'slip of a girl.' For as long as Peggy had known her, she had always looked the same: old, withered, with scraggly gray hair and piercing gray eyes. Her clothes were old fashioned, high-necked long gray or black dresses, and she always wore black leather boots with little black buttons. She smelled like the sea, of wild heather, and of herbs and spices.

"It was past midnight when I was walking these very cliffs," Granny continued. "I held my lantern low in fear that the revenue men would see it. They were always lurking about, spying."

"Revenue men are customs, or coastal police, right, Granny?" Peggy asked.

"Of a sort, child." Granny frowned. "Now don't you go asking me questions all the time. Do you want to hear the story or not?" She sat up straighter and looked as though she was going to get up. "Maybe I won't be telling it to you now."

"Sorry, Granny," Peggy muttered. She sat still, hoping that Granny would continue. Minutes passed.

Granny nodded her approval. "Now, like I was telling you, I was holding the lantern low, and I was wishing hard that nothing would go wrong. Then I heard sounds filling the night air. At first, I thought it was the wind whistling through the rock tunnels, or the sea calling, but no. True as I sit here, Peggy, it was them I was hearing, and when I came up to these very rocks, right where we are now, I saw *them*." Granny Poldune's voice lowered to a raspy whisper. "Shadowy shapes, above me, below me, all around me. I've never seen the like before, nor since, I can tell you that. The moon hid itself behind a cloud and I raised my lantern to see them better. Golden they were with silver eyes, Peggy. Can you imagine that? Silver eyes!"

Peggy felt a shiver run up and down her spine. "Were they Cornish Piskies?"

Granny shook her head. "No, Peggy, but they've been called that amongst other things." She straightened her shoulders and turned to look into Peggy's eyes. "Who I saw that night, Peggy, were the mystical beings of the Cornish coast, rarely seen, and gifted with great powers." Granny's eyes shone with pride. "Dancing they were, weaving through the air like silken thread. And their voices were like the sound of the tiniest silver bells. Why, the very sound of them made me so happy inside of myself, I was fit to burst, but they made me forget what I was doing there on the cliffs at midnight. They made me forget the trust I carried."

Granny stopped speaking. She turned away and closed her eyes. Peggy couldn't stand to wait another second. "What happened, Granny," she cried.

Granny opened her eyes and said in a low voice, "I tried to see them better. I raised my lantern, Peggy. I forgot that I had to keep that lantern low."

"But you said the revenue men were spying on you, Granny. Did they catch you?"

"Yes! There was a terrible pounding of great boots

behind me. Scared the wits out of me. I heard the shouts of the revenue men. I swear my heart almost stopped with the fright of it." Granny bent over, her hand on her chest.

'What happened then?" Peggy demanded. She pulled at the sleeve of the old woman's black cardigan.

Granny sat up, and when she opened her eyes, they were sparkling with merriment. She cackled with pleasure. "It wasn't me, the child with the lantern, they were after. It was my old grandfather they wanted, and fools that they were, they thought my raised lantern was the signal he was waiting for. They went down to the cove to hide behind the rocks and boulders so they could pounce on him when he came ashore with his bounty."

"Did they get him, Granny?"

"Bless you, child, no. A lantern waving about on the cliffs would never have fooled the old salt. Unless he saw the light circle thrice, stop, then circle thrice again, he'd stay at sea, but I would have given that signal if I had not raised my lantern to see them better. They saved us all that night. And as for them revenue devils, they huddled down in the cove all night long, cramping their bones," Granny cackled again.

The little brown rabbit bounded out from between Granny's boots, kicked up his hind legs, and scampered away. "Time to get back, Peggy," Granny said, standing up and smoothing down her dress. "I've work to be busy on."

Peggy linked her arm in Granny's as they walked back across the cliff top. From time to time, Granny Poldune darted forward, and reached into the depths of the sprouting heather and sea pink clusters. Triumphantly, she held aloft tiny plants Peggy had never seen before, plants with strange, green spiky leaves. "Are these for your special ointments and potions, Granny?" Peggy asked.

"I don't hold with spying, Peggy Tregarth," Granny muttered crossly.

Peggy murmured a quick apology. Granny was very secretive about her homemade remedies. They usually had a pungent odor, but they had more healing power than anything her mother bought from the chemist.

As they walked, Peggy thought about the story Granny had just told her. "Do you think the legend is true, Granny? About the Piskies, I mean."

Granny snorted. "Legend? Didn't I just tell you I've seen them? Legend indeed."

"I mean about them granting people wishes and bringing good luck," Peggy said quickly. At times, Granny could be as prickly as a gorse bush.

Granny stopped walking and peered sharply at her. "Wishes is it? And do you think you've been deserving of a wish from them you are calling the Piskies? For the life of me, I don't know another name, nor have I heard of another name spoken." She shrugged her shoulders. "No matter," she said. "Piskies it shall be. Well then, answer me, child. Do you think you deserve a wish from the Piskies?"

"I suppose not," answered Peggy. If she could make a wish, she would wish for Tor, her wild stallion. "Um, I was just wondering if you know about it," she added.

"Know about it? Of course I know about it," Granny answered indignantly. Her voice changed to a singsong chant.
"The gift must be given before the clock strikes eleven.
The wish must be made by half-past seven.
Tell that wish to a living soul,
Sure as death, it will fall afoul."
Granny's voice returned to its normal pitch. "The Piskies decide first if they'll take the gift. If they do, a big magic

circle will appear. It is in this circle that they'll hear the wish, but that don't mean they'll grant it. Their ways are strange. Piskies are kin to the wild animals and birds of the cliffs and fields, and can be just as unpredictable. Never can tell what they'll do, you see."

"But do you know anybody who made a wish for something, and actually got it, Granny?" Peggy persisted. "I know they helped you to save your grandfather that night, but do you know anyone who asked for something unusual and got it?"

Granny frowned. "You must have good reason to bother the Piskies, Peggy. They will judge you. If they find you lacking, you could be marked. Piskies can read a body's mind."

"Dad says Piskies are full of mischief. They play tricks on mean people, turn the cows' milk sour if you don't put out cream for them, and they open gates to let the horses and cows out." Peggy giggled. "Dad said it was the Piskies who opened the heifer gate. They trampled on all of Mum's camellias in the garden."

Granny laughed and startled a gull from her nest in a nook near the edge of the cliffs. The large gray and white bird swooped into the sky, screeching her complaint at being disturbed. "They'll do that and more," she said.

Granny looked out to sea and her face changed from good humor to anger. Peggy followed her gaze and saw Scottish purse seiners casting their nets. "Foreigners," Granny muttered. She turned abruptly and walked on.

Peggy grinned. If you weren't Cornish, you were a foreigner. Everybody knew that. She watched the purse seiners for a moment and then ran to catch up with Granny. They walked on towards home. Peggy's mind was still on the Piskies. Was wanting a stallion a good reason to bother the Piskies? Probably not. Then she remembered something else she had read about the Piskies in a book on the folklore of Cornwall. "Maybe what I read somewhere is right, Granny. Piskies are really souls who are not good enough to go to Heaven, but not bad enough to go to the devil."

"Do you think a soul has silver eyes and weaves through the air in a magic dance, Pegeen Tregarth?" Granny Poldune demanded.

Peggy didn't answer. When Granny called her Pegeen, she was cross with her. Besides, she didn't know what color eyes a soul had, if a soul had eyes at all. Was a soul the same as a ghost? Did the book mean that Piskies were ghosts? Peggy didn't think she would bother them after all, even for Tor.

Granny felt her discomfort. Her gray eyes were warm as she smiled at Peggy. "Ah, Peggy, folks put all mysterious things down to the dead. I've heard tell of this before, but I have my own notion." She looked around to make sure they were not being overheard, and stepped closer. "Before man they came," she whispered hoarsely, "and 'twas not on earth they were born at all. I'll say no more, Peggy. I'll say no more."

Peggy bit back the questions that raced into her mind. When Granny Poldune said she would say no more, she couldn't be persuaded otherwise. Granny was so hard to understand sometimes, and she said the strangest things, but as she stood there, gazing out to sea, she seemed to be a part of the cliffs, of the ocean, of all special things.

Without speaking, they walked the rest of the way across the cliffs until they reached the path Peggy must take to go home. Peggy was reluctant to leave Granny today. She stood on one foot, and then the other. It was Granny who spoke first. "Minded me about the fox?"

"Yes," Peggy answered. "I did just what you said."

When Granny smiled her approval, Peggy impulsively threw her arms around her. "Thank you, Granny. I don't think I could love my own granny, even if I had one, as much as I love you."

A tear trickled down the old woman's cheek. Quickly she brushed it away. "Darn old wind up here," she muttered gruffly. "Stings the eyes it does."

Peggy hugged her again, turned, and ran down the mud path. Granny was the best. Although she didn't know her own grandmothers, they couldn't be better than Granny Poldune. Her mother's mother had died when she was three, and her father's mother had died before she was even born. That was okay, though, because she had Granny Poldune and Granny Poldune was definitely the best granny in the whole world.

As Peggy jumped over the stone stile and raced across the heifer field, she hoped she could get to Chyoak before her mother got in from the fields. It was getting dark, but Mum always worked until after the sun went down. Peggy ducked under the clotheslines. Maybe she should take down the wash and fold it. It would be much better for her if her mother didn't know that she had gone to the cliffs.

Peggy turned the doorknob of the cottage door, and tried to push it open, but the door wouldn't open. Something was caught under it. Peggy pushed harder, kicking the obstruction out of the way. Irritated, she glanced down to see what it was, and gasped in horror. Her stomach turned somersaults. An old horseshoe, bound in faded purple wool, was lying just inside the doorway.

Chapter Three

Tregarth's Good Luck

Peggy stared down at the old horseshoe, unwilling to believe her eyes. What was it doing on the floor? She had kicked it! But who had put it there? Then she remembered the odd clunking sound she had heard earlier when she had left the cottage. It was her fault! She had slammed the door so hard, she had knocked the Tregarth's lucky horseshoe off its nails. Her mother and her father were going to kill her for that! Everything they did depended upon how lucky their horseshoe was that day. When things went well, they always gave credit to the horseshoe.

Gingerly, Peggy picked up the horseshoe and put it on the kitchen table. She looked at the door where it had always hung, long before she had been born. Her father had painted the door a light gray last summer. In the center, there was a dark brown horseshoe shape, smeared with cream, yellow, light green, and dark green paint. She remembered the door being brown and green, but she didn't know it had been painted all those other colors.

Her fingers trembled as she traced around the flaking brown paint, starting at one end, down, around the curve, and back up. Her father, grandfather, and great grandfather, who had hung it there, would not take the horseshoe down to paint the door. Tregarth's good luck lived within the curve of the horseshoe.

A sense of urgency gripped her. She grabbed the nails from the floor, and hammered them back in with the heel of her shoe. She tested them. They were still loose. She ran into the scullery to get the small hammer, used for cracking lobster and crab claws, and tapped the nails in more securely. "Now the horseshoe," she muttered. It was heavy. "Dad should have made sure the nails were holding you on properly," she said, tucking a stray strand of wool into the weave. It's not my fault you fell off."

She remembered her mother shouting through the window every morning, "Stop slamming that door!"

"One time too many," she whispered. She carefully jammed the old horseshoe back in its place and studied it to make sure it looked the same. One of the top nails looked too long. Peggy gave all seven of them another firm tap with the hammer.

Peggy stepped back from the horseshoe and looked at it critically. Good. It looked the same as it always had. Nobody would ever know it had fallen. She tapped the base of the horseshoe with the tip of her fingers, just as her father did, without fail, every time he went to sea. The horseshoe became blurred.

Choking back a sob, Peggy picked up Nimbob who had been watching her with interest from his favorite place on the window seat. She buried her face in his fur. "It looks the same, Nimby, but it's not the same at all. Tregarth's Good Luck must never, ever, be turned upside down." She hugged her cat tighter. "Now it's been on the floor for hours. We're doomed, Nimby, doomed forever, and it's all my fault!"

"There you are, Peggy," Jean Tregarth said briskly. She

closed the cottage door and hurried into the scullery. "Did you get my note? I was hoping I'd see you in the daffodil fields." Peggy didn't answer. She stayed on the window seat, hugging Nimbob, deciding whether or not to tell her mother. If she told her, she would be so angry, and then she would tell Dad! Her mother put the kettle on for tea. "I've never seen our Alfreds look like this. King Alfreds are getting a good price at the markets this year. No matter what I do for them, they still don't look like they should." She banged the frying pan on the stove. "Peggy?"

Peggy looked up at her mother, who was standing in the doorway of the scullery. She hesitated. Maybe she should just tell her. "Mum, I ..." She held Nimbob closer for courage.

"Stop playing with that cat and dreaming your life away. I never knew such an irresponsible child! The wash won't bring itself in. I don't know what's got into you lately. Now when I was twelve, I was a help to my mother. She could depend on me, but you..."

Peggy put Nimbob down and stumbled past her mother. She jerked the wicker laundry basket off the peg by the back door, ran through the kitchen and out of the front door. How could she tell her mother anything when she was shouting at her like that? Mum was mad at her because she hadn't gone to the fields to help, but she didn't want to do it anymore. Didn't Mum know that? She had given her enough clues, but Mum never listened to her. Every year since she was four years old, she had helped to bunch the daffodils. Dad had teased her about it. He always said that it was the daffodils that had taught her to count. When she was older, she had worked in the fields, helping to weed, and then picked hundreds of the yellow flowers every year.

Peggy threw clothes pegs into a bag hanging from the line and began tossing the wash into the basket. Knocking down Tregarth's Good Luck was an accident. She hadn't meant to do it. Peggy pressed her face into a white cotton towel billowing in the breeze. "Smells like the sea," she whispered and felt better.

When her mother placed a piece of fried mackerel with two slices of bread and butter on a white china plate in front of her, Peggy wrinkled her nose in disgust. She was about to complain when she saw the look on her mother's face. Her mother's lips were a thin line. Her blue-green eyes were cold and distant. Peggy picked up her knife and fork. She used to love fried mackerel, but every day? It's probably why I have those two pimples on my forehead, she thought resentfully. Too much fried fish.

"When you've finished, Peggy, you can do the dishes." Her mother sighed and pushed herself up from the table as though she was too heavy for herself.

Peggy looked up at her. Mum usually looks pretty, she thought. Tonight her brown hair hung limply to her shoulders and her face was pale. There were dark shadows under her eyes. "Are you sick, Mum?" she asked with concern.

"No, no, Peggy. I'm fine. Just a worry or two, that's all."

Relieved, Peggy cleared the table and took the dishes into the scullery. Her mother went into the sitting room. Peggy filled the sink with hot water and put the dishes in. She looked at the clock. It was past six. It was finally time. She ran into the sitting room. Her mother was sitting on the floral couch, looking through the sewing box for the right shade of yarn. A pile of her father's thick woolen socks was beside her. "It's past six, Mum. Remember I told you Granny said I could check on the fox after six?"

"After the dishes," her mother replied.

"Do I have to wash and dry them?" Peggy asked.

"All two plates, cups, and saucers!" her mother snapped.

It only took a few minutes to do the dishes, but Peggy couldn't wait to get out of the scullery and go into the yard. It had been hard to obey Granny Poldune. She had wanted to go and see how the fox was doing several times, but Granny had said she had to wait until after six o'clock tonight.

Would he be alive or dead? Would he be foaming at the mouth, with red eyes, mad from the rabies? Peggy reached for the second plate to dry. It slipped from her hands onto the stone floor.

"Are you all right, Peg?" her mother asked.

"Yes, sorry. I dropped a plate," Peggy replied. Her mother didn't answer.

Peggy grabbed the broom and dustpan from the cupboard and quickly swept up the broken china. She dumped it in the rubbish bin. "I'm going to see the fox now, Mum," she said, as she came back into the kitchen. "The dishes are done and I swept up the plate bits."

"Are you sure you got all of it?" her mother asked.

"I got it all, Mum," Peggy replied as she went back into the scullery, down the passage, turned on the yard light, and went out of the back door.

"I wish you would stop bringing home sick animals, Peggy. They're full of vermin and diseases," her mother shouted after her.

Peggy flinched. Her mother had really changed. Not so long ago she would have come out with her to see how the fox was doing. Last spring, they had raised a litter of orphaned wild rabbits together. They were tiny and helpless when she had found them, but with her mother's help, every one of them had lived to scamper off into the fields. Peggy had buried the mother rabbit. Someone had shot her. "I hope I don't have to bury you, Mr. Fox," she whispered, as she approached the chicken wire pen they had built for the rabbits.

The fox was on his feet when Peggy reached the pen. Delighted, Peggy watched him. His amber eyes were a lot like Nimbob's eyes, except they were scared, trapped eyes. His bushy tail hung between his rear legs and his slender furry body was tense. How different he looked tonight from when she had found him, lying in the lane leading to Chyoak. She had thought he was dead at first, but his ears were twitching. Peggy had dropped her backpack and had run to the flower shed to get a potato sack. Wrapping the sack around the fox's slack body, Peggy had carried him to the pen. Then she had run to the cove to ask Granny Poldune what to do.

Peggy had found Granny collecting pieces of seaweed from the rocks. Quickly she explained her mission. "You shouldn't have touched him," Granny Poldune had scolded her. "You can never tell if a fox is vicious. And if he was dead, your mother wouldn't thank you for the parcel of fleas you'd be bringing into the house. Well, seeing as you've already gone and done it, you'd best leave him be until six o'clock tomorrow night. Mind me," she added sternly. "Don't go near that fox until then. If he's not up and about, but still alive, I'll come."

The fox was not just up and about, but quivering in his need to escape the confines of the pen. Peggy smiled. He looked just fine now. She didn't need to go to the cove and bring Granny back to help him. Last night, at teatime, she had asked her parents what they thought had happened to him. After they had both told her off thoroughly for touching the wild animal, her father had said that he thought the fox was probably old and sick, and was looking for a place he could die in peace. She didn't want to finish her meal after her father had said that.

Nimbob stalked the fox, hiding behind a large, pink, rhododendron. He pounced forward, instantly retreating when the fox made the slightest movement. "I see you have that fox covered, Nimby," Peggy said with a laugh. Nimbob did not like people laughing at him. He ignored her, swung his sleek tail in a circle, and jumped up on the stonewall behind the pen. As though to prove to Peggy that he had no concerns whatsoever about that fox, he turned his back on them.

The fox took short, quick steps to one side of the pen, sniffed the ground, and ran to the other side of the pen. Peggy chuckled as she came closer. "You prefer chicken pens with chickens in them, don't you, Mr. Fox?" The fox backed away. "Don't worry, I'll set you free," Peggy said in a soothing voice. She pulled up the wooden latch holding the pen door closed and moved off to the side. The door swung open. Suspicious, the fox was still; his long nose sniffed the air. Only his whiskers were twitching. Then he was gone - a red-gray streak in the grass.

Peggy skipped back into the cottage. "He's fine, Mum," she said excitely. "I let him go."

Her mother nodded. "Good," she said. "Now let that be the end of it."

Nimbob rubbed against Peggy's legs. "Hungry?" Peggy asked. "I saved mackerel scraps for you." She went back into the scullery and fed the cat. "When you are done, I'll give you some milk," she said.

Peggy went into the sitting room and perched on the edge of her father's armchair, a match to the floral sofa. She looked at the television. The screen was blank. Her mother always watched the news and the weather report after tea. Peggy scowled. "Mum, didn't Dad fix the telly yet?"

Her mother was weaving a light brown pattern of wool where the heel of her father's work sock had once been. She did not look up from her work. "Jack Treseder came by and took a look at it yesterday."

"Can he fix it, Mum?" Peggy asked eagerly. The television had been broken forever. She hadn't really missed it because of all the studying she had to do for the end of term exams. All winter long she had spent most of her evenings doing homework in her room. Now she could catch up on all of her favorite programs. "Mum, did you hear me?"

"We'll see," said her mother, snipping the yarn with her small sewing scissors.

"When will Mr. Treseder be coming back?" Peggy demanded. Her mother picked up another sock and sighed. She slipped the darning spool down to the heel and started to sew. "Mum, when is Jack Treseder coming back to fix the telly?" Peggy asked again.

"When he can," her mother answered curtly.

"Didn't he say when he was coming?" Peggy persisted.

"He didn't say," her mother replied, bent over her work. "A cup of tea would be welcome, Peggy."

"Mum, can I go meet Dad? He's late tonight." Peggy got up and went to the window. She drew back the green check curtains and peered out.

"Not tonight," her mother replied.

"Why not?" Peggy demanded.

"Because I said so," her mother said quietly. "Please put the kettle on for tea."

Peggy went to the scullery, filled the electric kettle, and switched it on. Mum was mean. Dad loved it when she met him in the cove. He always smiled his happiest smile when he saw her on the slip waiting for him. He said she was his best catch of the day. Tonight was important. She couldn't wait to see him. With no school, she could make plans to go out in the boat with him and pull the lobster and crab pots.

Nimbob mewed plaintively in the doorway. "Want your milk now?" Peggy asked. She took a small carton of milk from the refrigerator and poured some of it into Nimbob's bowl. She bent down and set it on the floor. Nimbob stayed in the doorway, mewing. He lifted his right front paw. Peggy frowned. Nimbob always ran to his bowl when there was milk in it. What was wrong with his paw?

Peggy picked up the cat. When she looked at his paw, she saw a sliver of white china imbedded in the pink pad. Blood dripped onto her hand. "Nimby, I'm sorry," she cried, hurrying to the cupboard where her mother kept the medical supplies. Still holding the cat, she grabbed the antiseptic spray, and set it on the countertop. Using her nails, she pulled the china splinter from Nimbob's paw and sprayed the injury. Nimbob leaped from her arms in alarm and ran from the room, lashing his tail.

Peggy's relieved smile left her face when she heard her mother cry, "Get out from under my feet, Cat!"

Her mother ran into the scullery. Her left hand was dripping blood. "I've jabbed the stupid darning needle right under my nail," she cried, her face pinched with pain. She opened the cupboard to find the antiseptic spray.

"It's here, Mum," Peggy said. "Let me spray it on for you."

"I can do that myself, thank you," her mother said in a tight voice. "Where's the plasters?" She fumbled when she opened the box and the contents spilled onto the floor.

Peggy knelt to pick them up. "Does it hurt a lot?" she asked anxiously.

Her mother chose a large plaster from the box and applied it to her nail. "It'll be fine. I should have been more careful," she said. "I'm not usually that clumsy. Just a bit of bad luck, that's all."

Peggy winced at her mother's words. She made her mother a cup of tea. Bad things were happening already, she thought. First Nimby, now Mum. Who would be next? She added a spoon of sugar to the hot tea and gave the cup to her mother, who was sitting at the kitchen table. I'd better warn her, Peggy decided. Most things need a little luck, but their lucky horseshoe wasn't lucky any more. "Mum, I have to tell you something."

"What is it now?" her mother said, cradling her left hand. "If it's bad news I don't want to hear it. I've had all I can stomach for this day."

Peggy looked out of the kitchen window. It was bad news. Maybe she should wait for a better time to tell her mother. It was too dark to see anything outside. Why wasn't Dad home? She was beginning to worry about him. Peggy glanced at her mother, but she was doing the cross-word puzzle in the newspaper. Her mother chewed the end of her pencil. "A five letter word," she muttered. She picked up her cup of tea with her left hand and cried out. The cup fell and hot tea spilled all over the newspaper. Peggy watched her mother run to get a kitchen towel. More bad luck, she thought, as she helped her mother to clean up the mess.

Her father had still not come home when Peggy reluctantly went to bed. Her mother had insisted upon it and had told Peggy that she was in no mood for an argument. Peggy had stood on the bottom step of the stairs and gazed at Tregarth's Good Luck. Maybe she was imagining it, but it didn't look friendly anymore. "I shouldn't have hung you back up," she whispered. "You're bringing us bad luck now."

Even though it was too dark outside to see the path, Peggy peered out of her bedroom window to see if her father was coming. Finally she gave up and went to the bathroom to wash, brush her teeth, and get ready for bed. It had been a long day and Peggy was really tired. She switched off her light and climbed into bed, pulling the covers up to her neck. Peggy didn't put her earphones on and turn on her music as she usually did when she got into bed. Tonight she wanted to be sure she heard her father when he came home. She still had that weird feeling in the pit of her stomach. There was no doubt about it. She had to tell her parents about Tregarth's Good Luck falling...and, she bit her lip, that she had kicked it. They had to know about it so they could watch out and avoid accidents. They couldn't depend on good luck any more – only bad.

Peggy pulled the pillow over her head. If only she could go back to this afternoon. She would close the door gently. There would be no clunking sound as the horseshoe fell. None of what happened would happen. And if she had gone right back into the cottage when she had heard it fall, she could have saved some of the good luck from falling out. But she couldn't go back. She couldn't change it!

The cottage door opened and Peggy heard the sound of her father's voice. She sighed with relief. She couldn't bear it if anything had happened to him, but Dad was okay. He was home, safe and sound.

"Well?" she heard her mother ask.

"Sixteen mackerel all day," her father said in a disgusted voice.

Peggy sat up. Sixteen mackerel? What kind of catch was that? She must have heard it wrong.

"We can't go on like this," her mother said in a worried voice.

"Joe Chapple was at the meeting tonight. He said the petition was being heard and they would more than likely put a ban on the big boats. It's the Scots who got my fish today and that's a fact."

"Who else was there?" her mother asked him.

"Oh, just about everybody we know, and then some. Trevor Vernon wanted to fight the Scots." Her father chuckled. "He said we should punch their lights out and he put up his fists, and started boxing the air. Willie Hawkins got all excited and jumped up. Vernon bopped him one right on the nose. Gave us all a laugh that did."

"Was Willie hurt?" her mother asked, concerned.

"A bloody nose is all," her father said, and chuckled again. "You should have seen the look on his face, though. I was laughing all the way home remembering the look on Willie's face."

"What's so funny about that?" her mother asked crossly. "Poor old Willie."

"Oh, he's all right, Jean," her father said, his voice now sounding tired. "Things were getting too tense by far, and Willie's bloody nose broke the tension. Is there any supper? I'm as hungry as a horse."

Her parents went into the scullery and Peggy couldn't

hear more than an odd word or two. She thought about what she had overheard. Dad had only caught sixteen mackerel. Peggy yawned. Dad's catch was so small, it wasn't enough to even bother taking to Newlyn Market. All the time she was worrying about him, he had been at a meeting. Peggy slipped out of bed and retrieved her pillow. She climbed back into bed. Dad was home safe and sound, and that was all that mattered right now. She drifted into a deep sleep.

Chapter Four

Peggy's Secret Cave

With a cry, Peggy sat up in bed. Sunlight streamed into her window. She looked at the time on the clock on her bedside table. It was eight o'clock. Why hadn't Mum called her? She'd be late for school. The bus would leave without her!

Peggy lay back down with a grin. No, it wouldn't. It was Saturday. Not only that, it was the first day of her holidays. She didn't have to get up early today. In fact, she didn't have to get up early for three whole weeks!

The grin left her face as parts of her dream came back to her. In the dream, she was with her father at sea. They were in *The Sunrise*. "Your turn to haul the lines," her father had said, but all the mackerel on her line of hooks jumped back into the water. Clunking sounds like thunder filled the air. She had looked to her father for help, but she was alone in the boat. She had felt angry at all the escaping fish. She leaned over the boat and grabbed one. It wasn't a fish at all. It was an old horseshoe, bound in faded purple wool. It felt slimy and, as she held it, it moved in her hands. The clunking sounds grew even louder as the horseshoe changed into a horrible, evil face.

Shuddering, Peggy jumped out of bed. She didn't want to remember any more of that horrible nightmare. She ran to her window. The sky was a bright blue, filled with white, puffy clouds. The clouds were playing tag, chasing each other in the early morning breeze.

"Pegeen Tregarth, are you going to sleep all day?" her mother called from the foot of the stairs.

"Coming, Mum," Peggy yelled, running into the bathroom to splash cold water on her face. Quickly, she brushed her hair. She turned to go back to her bedroom, when she remembered the pimples. She peered into the mirror. They looked bigger, she thought in dismay. Huge!

She dressed in her jeans and yellow jumper, and ran downstairs. She avoided looking up at the back of the cottage door. "I'm starved," she said.

Her mother placed a bowl of steaming porridge in front of her as she slid into her seat at the kitchen table. "I'll need your help today in the fields, Peggy."

Peggy made a face. "Porridge again?" she asked. "I'd like bacon and scrambled eggs, Mum."

Her mother didn't reply. She tied a gray patterned headscarf around her head and pulled on her old brown work coat. "It looks like a nice day out, but there's a stiff breeze blowing," she said as she left the cottage.

Peggy sprinkled sugar over her porridge and poured some milk into the center. She stirred it with a spoon until it was exactly the way she liked it. Nimbob jumped up onto her lap, purring. "Forgiven me, Nimby?" she asked, tickling him under his chin. Nimbob revved his engine. She turned over his front paw. The pad was a little swollen, but not bleeding any more.

As she ate, she realized that she should have asked her mother about her thumb. It looked as though it had really hurt her last night. Well, she didn't give me the chance, she thought crossly. She was out of the door two seconds after I got here. All she ever does is fuss over the stupid daffodils.

Peggy took her empty dish out to the sink in the scullery, and ran back up to her room to put on her socks and trainers. Before she went to the daffodil fields, she wanted to run down to the beach and get something from her cave. She wouldn't have a chance to do it once she went to work on the daffodils. There had been a storm a couple of days ago and the seas had been really high. Peggy hoped that everything would be safe.

Peggy ran downstairs and reached for the cottage door-knob. Apprehensive, she looked up at Tregarth's Good Luck. It was just an old horseshoe. It didn't look anything like it had in her dream. Still, after she had gone to her cave, she would find Granny Poldune. She had to reverse what she had done. Granny would know what to do.

The air smelled of the awakening earth, fresh grasses, spring flowers, and as always, of the sea. She would only be gone for an hour or so, she told herself, and then she would go and help her mother.

Peggy had to cross the cliffs to get to Pedneyvounder Beach. She was always worrying about somebody finding her cave and the treasures she had hidden there. She had decided to move her personal items to her cave after she had found that her things were not exactly in the same place as she had left them in her room. Suspicious, she had asked her mother if she had gone through her things, but her mother had denied it. What she had said, though, was that she had cleaned the room. She had also given Peggy a long lecture about how messy her room was. The next day Peggy went to the cave to hide her treasures.

Shading her eyes, Peggy looked out to sea before she

made her way down the steep path to the beach. The water was silvery in the pale sunshine, and the wind whipped the waves into ridges. Big trawlers and Scottish purse seiners filled the skyline. There were a lot of big boats in Mounts Bay, fishing the miles of mackerel shoals in her waters.

Pedneyvounder's white shell sand was wet and gritty under Peggy's bare feet. She had stuffed her socks into her trainers, tied the shoelaces together, and swung her trainers over her left shoulder. Peggy saw an unbroken shell glinting on a rock. She slipped it into the pocket of her jeans. Peggy walked across the beach to the cliff on the other side. There was nobody on the beach today. It was too cold. Even so, she climbed to the left, and then to the right, just in case somebody was watching her. She was quick in her step when she climbed passed a gull's nest on a ledge in a sheltered spot. She hoped the mother gull was not about with her protective, sharp beak.

Peggy grinned as she looked back down at the nest. It would be brilliant if the gull that had built the nest, close to her secret cave, was one of the gulls she had helped to save when the beaches were covered in sticky black oil. A tanker had sunk in another part of the Atlantic and the currents had brought the oil to the Cornish coastline. A lot of sea-gulls were covered in oil and couldn't fly. It was Granny Poldune who had helped her to clean their feathers with a detergent solution, and they had flown away with raucous cries. It was definitely one of the happiest days in her life.

She crawled into the small entrance to the cave that was hidden by a large granite rock that jutted out of the cliff. Seaweed, broken shells, and debris littered the entrance, but as she crawled further in, the sand was dry. Her hiding place at the back of the cave had not been disturbed. Relieved,

Peggy removed the large tin box that had once held biscuits. There was a picture of Queen Elizabeth on the lid. Peggy crawled back closer to the entrance so she could see and opened the box. She found what she was looking for on the bottom in a corner. It was a silver chain with a Cornish Piskie charm on it. She examined it carefully. She had found it on the cliffs one day, close to Logan Rock. The catch was broken on the chain, so she couldn't wear it. When Peggy put the chain into her jeans' pocket, she found the shell. It was a pretty white shell. It's like a pearl, she decided, adding it to her growing collection in the old tin box.

Peggy took her small, red diary from the box, and hunted for her pen. She usually read the last entry before she added another, but she had no time today. She muttered the words she wrote aloud. "Yesterday I knocked Tregarth's Good Luck off its nails, and then I kicked it! I'm worried about the bad luck we might get now. It has already started with accidents. Dad's catch was poor, too. I don't know what to do. I'm going to ask Granny Poldune to help me"

Peggy closed the diary and put it back into the tin. The white paper bag inside the tin was sticky. She opened it and pried a large humbug free. As she sucked on the brown and white peppermint, she considered how she should tell Granny. It wasn't going to be easy. Granny Poldune had no time for careless people. She had no choice, though. She had to risk Granny's disapproval. There was nobody else she could turn to.

Peggy put the bag of sweets away and closed the tin. The Queen of England smiled up at her. She would love to see the queen in person, but London was close to three hundred miles away. Maybe one day she would get to see her. Peggy crawled to the back of the cave, to the crevice in the rocks where she hid her treasure tin. She piled up some loose rocks to further conceal it. She made sure that the coast was clear before she climbed back down to the beach. As she climbed, Peggy wondered where Granny would be today. If she didn't meet her on the cliffs, she would go to the cove to Granny's cottage.

Chapter Five

Granny Poldune

Peggy ran across Pedneyvounder's deserted beach. At the foot of the cliff path, she brushed the sand from her feet and put her socks and trainers back on. She climbed back up the steep, rocky path to the cliff top.

She scanned the cliffs for Granny Poldune, but there was no sign of the familiar old woman. Mrs. Rogers, with her black Labrador, Prince, was walking towards her. Peggy petted the dog. "You'll be missing Pal still, right, Peggy?" Mrs. Rogers asked kindly. "Prince and Pal were just like twins. I loved to watch them play and romp about."

Peggy nodded. "We all miss him so much," she replied sadly. "We only lost him a year ago, but it seems like he has been gone forever."

Mrs. Rogers made sympathetic noises as she moved on in the opposite direction. Peggy hurried across the cliffs to the cove to find Granny. She saw Pal in her mind's eye. He was so handsome with a black, shiny coat. He tilted his head to one side, waiting for her to throw the tennis ball into the sea, his whole body quivering with anticipation. With a joyful bark, he raced after the ball, returning in seconds to drop it at her feet. Peggy felt the tears form in her eyes. "You were the best," she muttered. "You were the best dog in the whole world!"

Her father had said they should have named Pal "Shadow" because he rarely left Peggy's side. Pal roamed the cliffs and beaches with her, and was always waiting for her in the lane when she came home from school. At night, he lay beside her bed. She didn't mind when he snored. Knowing he was there made her feel safe. Sometimes Peggy missed him so much, the missing became a pain in her chest.

Peggy climbed down the steep path to the cove. "Please be there, Granny," she muttered aloud. The cove was quiet. There were a couple of boats pulled up on the cobbled slip, but *The Sunrise* was not there. A hand liner was busy working on his boat that was turned upside down. He had stripped the boat and was opening a can of blue paint. An old man was sitting on the bench at the top of the slip, enjoying the sunshine. "Lovely day," he said to her as she passed him.

"Lovely day," echoed Peggy, her eyes fixed on Granny's cottage. Smoke spiraled from the chimney in the gray slate roof. It looked as though Granny was home.

Granny Poldune was sitting outside in an old wooden rocking chair. She was sorting through square pieces of different patterned fabric in a white cardboard shoebox, putting the pieces that matched in the lid of the box. Wire-rimmed glasses perched on the end of her nose. "Hello, Granny," Peggy said. "How are you?"

"I am as you see me, Peggy Tregarth," Granny said testily.

It was obvious to Peggy, who knew Granny well, that she didn't want company. She could leave and come back later. That would be the polite thing to do. But if she did that, how would she know what to do?

Granny clucked her tongue in irritation, put the matching pieces of fabric back in the box, and put the lid on. "You've come to tell me about the fox?"

Peggy grinned. "Mr. Fox was just fine, Granny. He ran off into the fields."

Granny nodded. "Saw your dad go out early this morning. Wished him luck, I did. He's going to need that with the way things are."

It was the opening that Peggy needed. Granny had mentioned luck herself, but she was still not sure how to tell Granny what she had done. She sat on a large boulder beside the old woman. She cleared her throat. "Granny, if a person wrecked her good luck, how long would that person have bad luck?"

"That depends on what the person did," Granny said. She stopped rocking and looked at Peggy. "Luck, good and bad, is not something to be trifled with."

"I know," Peggy said.

"Fair enough," Granny said. "If you know you must respect it, it won't be too bad."

"But it is, Granny, it is!"

"You'd best tell me all about it then," Granny said. "Go on. Out with it."

"I ...I knocked down my family's horseshoe, Tregarth's Good Luck. My great grandfather hung it on the back of the cottage door, and it has always been there, but I slammed the door. Then I didn't know it was on the floor and I kicked it."

Granny Poldune pursed her lips. She was silent for a moment or two. Peggy held her breath. Then Granny spoke. "Was it a horseshoe found in dawn's early light, cast off by a wild horse, that had been caught, but broke free by luck and spirit? And was that horseshoe then bound in thick wool to cover every inch of it, and hung in one place?"

Peggy frowned. She didn't know when or where her great grandfather had found the horseshoe, but it was bound in purple wool, and had always hung in the same place.

Peggy nodded slowly. "I think so, Granny."

"This is the horseshoe you were so careless with, Peggy?" Granny asked, her voice sharp.

Peggy swallowed hard, and nodded again. "It was an accident. I didn't know it would fall off its nails, Granny. I slammed the cottage door, and the horseshoe fell off, but I put it back. The problem is I didn't put it back right away, then I kicked it, and now bad luck has come into our cottage. Mum had an accident with the darning needle, Nimbob hurt his paw, and I think it's the horseshoe that's bringing us bad luck now instead of good luck. What do you think?"

"Take that horseshoe down, Peggy, wrap it in silver paper, and bury it where it will bring no harm," Granny said firmly.

Peggy gasped. She couldn't take the family's horseshoe down, and bury it. Her parents would be furious with her if she did that. She needed to know how to fix it, not bury it! A groan escaped her lips.

Granny put a hand on her shoulder. "To tell you the truth, Peggy, I don't think that old horseshoe had much luck left to give. Luck comes and goes. But what you did to it, after it has been helping your family for all those years, would be a sign of ingratitude. Ingratitude, Peggy, is what you gave in return for all its years of service to you and yours. Bad luck is bound to follow."

Peggy nodded in agreement. She knew that already.

Now she needed to know if her idea would work. She pulled the silver chain from her pocket, and held it up for Granny to see. "What if I hang a Cornish Piskie on the horseshoe, Granny? Will that reverse the bad luck?"

Granny looked at the charm. She shook her head. "Not powerful enough," she said decidedly, and got up from her rocking chair. "I have to go in now. I've work to be busy on."

"But Granny, please, please tell me what to do!" The old woman didn't answer her. She went into her small cottage and closed the door.

Peggy scowled at the closed door. Granny had made her feel worse if that was possible. Slowly she turned, walked back over the rocks to the slip, and walked down to the water's edge. The seaweed was thick today, writhing in the waves like dark brown snakes. Peggy picked up a dry piece of weed from the slip and popped the bladders bulging on the flat surface. "He loves me," she said automatically for each bladder that made the pop sound. Most of them made the squish sound, but it didn't matter. She hadn't even said his name.

She picked up a small flat rock and skimmed it along the surface of the water. "Five skips," she said, and turned away.

Peggy walked back up the slip to the path. The old man on the bench beamed at her. "Lovely day," he said.

Chapter Six

Kings of the Sea

Peggy ran. The sun was high in the sky. Mum is going to ground me forever, she thought as she ran. I've disobeyed her two days in a row. I'll have to work extra hard in the fields to make up for it. She ran down the path to Chyoak to change into her Wellingtons. Her Nike trainers were new and she didn't want to ruin them in the muddy fields. She had begged her mother for them a month before she got them. Peggy only meant to spend a moment in the cottage, but to her surprise she found her father sitting at the kitchen table working on his lines. To Peggy's eyes, he always seemed to fill the space in the kitchen. Tall, and muscular, he had the weather-beaten face of a man who made his living from the sea. His hair was light brown, and his eyes, a bright blue. "Dad, why aren't you out fishing?" Peggy demanded.

"Engine trouble," her father said. "I barely got it into the boatyard at Newlyn. It kept spluttering and quitting on me. I couldn't believe it. I had it checked over only last month."

Peggy looked up at the horseshoe. She believed it. "Can they repair it?" she asked anxiously.

Her father nodded. He tied an orange feather hook onto his line. "I got a ride home with Theo Willis. He said he was putting his boat up for sale and getting out while the going was good."

"I know his daughter, Jill," Peggy said. "Are they moving?"

"Could be," said her father, now tying a red feather hook onto the line.

Peggy sat down at the kitchen table, upset by the news. "Mr. Willis is a hand liner like you, Dad."

"He is," her father replied.

"He's selling his boat?" Peggy's stomach began to churn.

"He's not the first, Peggy. There's rent to pay and food to put on the table," her father said, digging into his box of feathers. "Fishing isn't what it used to be, love."

"But you'd never sell *The Sunrise*, Dad, right?" Peggy asked.

Her father didn't answer. He tipped the box up on the table. "These are in a tangle sure enough," he said.

Peggy was about to pursue the subject when the headlines of a local paper lying on the chair next to her caught her attention. In bold capitals were the words "Kings of the Sea." Peggy picked up the newspaper and read the article. "Dad, they're saying here that the Scots are the kings of the sea!"

Her father grunted. "You'd think that reporter might think on it before he wrote that in our paper."

Peggy read on. The article described the purse seiner as a boat of about 120 feet long with a net large enough to cover a football stadium. In one hour, a purse seiner could catch a hundred tons of mackerel. There was even an electric fish finder on board the boat. When the Scots hauled in the fish, using heavy powered winches, they put hoses into the purse shaped net, and sucked all the fish into the seawater tanks below the deck.

She looked at her father, patiently putting the feathered hooks onto his line. He could only catch 30 fish a line if every hook was taken. When he pulled in his lines, he took the fish off by hand. Compared with those huge nets scooping up the mackerel like that, what chance did he have against the Scots? "Maybe you should go punch the Scots' lights out, like Mr. Vernon wanted to," she said, tossing the paper aside.

"How did you know about that?" he asked, a twinkle coming back into his eyes. "Fighting won't stop the problem, Peg. If we got into an altercation with them, what's to stop them mowing us down in our own waters? We've all been keeping out of their way to tell you the truth. None of us feel comfortable anywhere near them, and they are beginning to know the mackerel shoal paths as well as we do."

"Could they empty our sea?" Peggy asked.

"Now you've got it, Peg," her father said, pleased with her. "Those nets just suck up the fish. The breeding is bound to be affected. And the amount of fish being taken out of the sea is downright frightening."

Peggy thought about what he had said. "It'll be like the whales, Dad," she said. "We did a study on whale slaughter in school and lots of species of whales don't exist any more. But if the mackerel die out on our Cornish coast, what will the hand liners do?"

"They're doing it, Peg," her father said soberly. "Getting out like the Willis family. The small boats can't make a living from the sea like they used to. Still, there's a chance that the trawlers will be banned on conservation grounds. Maybe somebody will see that we have to save the shoals. Hope so, anyways. A cup of tea would go down nicely, Peg."

Peggy nodded and went into the scullery to put the kettle on. The words "Kings of the Sea" stayed in her mind. The Scots weren't the kings of the sea. Her father was the king of the Cornish sea, and foreigners had no right coming here and stealing his fish. Kings of the sea, indeed. The way those Scots were going, they would empty a kingdom that wasn't even theirs.

"Can you make your dad a sandwich?" her father called to her.

"Yes," Peggy answered. She found some bread, butter, and a jar of potted meat. She took two white china plates from the cupboard and two cups. As she made the lunch, she agonized over her all-important question to her father. Would he sell *The Sunrise* if the fishing didn't improve? She was sure that he hadn't answered her question because he couldn't bear to think of doing such a thing. His boat was his prize possession. He loved it even more than she did.

She heard the cottage door open and her mother's voice. "What are you doing here?" she asked in surprise.

Peggy heard her father explain about the boat engine and then he asked her how the daffodils were doing. She gripped the scullery sink when she heard her mother's reply. "Bill, you're not going to believe it. The whole crop is no good! It's the worst luck in the world. We've got eelworm."

Peggy turned to come into the kitchen. Her mother glanced at her as she stood in the scullery doorway, a horrified expression on her face. "Mum that's ..."

Her mother ignored her. "Come and take a look, Bill. I've brought some daffodils in with the bulbs on. They're in the shed. I want you to take a look at them." Her father got up and together they left the cottage. It was like she wasn't even there, Peggy thought, stung by her mother's rejection.

Needing something to do, Peggy made a sandwich for her mother and poured a third cup of tea. Getting eelworm was the worse luck yet. The nasty little worms buried into the daffodil bulbs and ate the goodness away.

Peggy carried the plates with the sandwiches on them into the kitchen. There was nowhere to put them. Fishing lines littered the table surrounded by hooks and brightly colored feathers. She carried the sandwiches back into the scullery.

She picked up her sandwich and took a bite. There were no fields of daffodils to pick any more. Now that she didn't have to work in the fields, that's what she wanted to do more than anything else in the world. She wanted to pick healthy, happy daffodils. Peggy sighed. Mum was so angry with her. She didn't even want to talk to her.

Nimbob rubbed against her legs. She poured some milk into his bowl, and knelt down to stroke him as his little pink tongue darted in and out of the milk. "The bad luck is getting worse," she confided.

Peggy finished her sandwich, drank her tea, and left her parents' lunches on the counter. She went upstairs to her room. There was so much she had to think about. She just had to do something to reverse all this bad luck. The problem was she didn't have a clue what to do.

Peggy stayed in her room most of the afternoon, and only came down when her mother called her for tea. Her parents hardly spoke to each other and neither spoke to her. Peggy was glad they were quiet. She couldn't stop thinking about the plan she had formulated in her room earlier. All afternoon she had thought about what she could do to stop the chaos that was building all around her, when suddenly, out of the blue, an idea came into her mind. The more she thought about it, the more excited she became.

She excused herself from the table and ran back up to her room. She took a school notebook and pencil from her backpack, and wrote down her idea. Then she wrote down what she would need to execute the plan. Money was first on the list. She would have to break into her china horse bank, but she was sure she had enough saved. Peggy wasn't sure about the second item. She needed to purchase something, but wasn't sure where to buy it. She hadn't bought any before. Her excitement grew as she wrote down the third item on her list. It was the location entry. The fourth item was the creative entry. The fifth item would be the proof of the pudding, as her mother always said.

Peggy read over what she had written several times. She had to work out the details. She had to do this right. Finally, she slipped the notebook under her pillow and lay down to think about it all some more. She was still struggling with her ideas when she fell asleep and was dreaming a nice dream about fishing with her father in *The Sunrise*. Suddenly the horrible clunking sounds started to pound in her ears. The sounds were so loud they made her feel as though her head was going to burst. The fish, their scales shining in the sunlight, leaped off their hooks and swam back into the water. Desperate, she grabbed the line and pulled it in. There was only one fish left on it. She reached for the fish and felt the slimy horseshoe shape move in her hands. Ugly worms with yellow eyes wriggled off the horseshoe onto her arms. They crawled up and up. The ugly purple shape moved up, too. Peggy screamed.

"Wake up, Peggy," her mother said, leaning over her bed. "You must be having a nightmare to be screaming like that. Get yourself into the shower, wash that unruly mop of hair, brush your teeth, and put on your pajamas. It's past your bedtime, and you'll need to be up early for church in the morning."

Peggy sat up groggily. She wanted her mother to hug her, but her mother had already left her room. Shivering, Peggy got up and went into the bathroom. It was hard to banish her dream from her mind. Obediently, she showered, washed her hair, brushed her teeth, and stared at herself in the mirror. That horseshoe had almost got her. If her mother had not woken her up, it would have devoured her! She would have disappeared into its slimy mouth.

When Peggy got back into bed, she didn't want to go to sleep. She pulled the covers over her head and went over the details of her plan again. It had to work and there was no doubt about it; she had to get rid of that evil horseshoe!

Peggy tossed and turned. She tried to go to sleep, but her fear of dreaming again about that horrible horseshoe kept her awake. What if her mother didn't hear her cry out and the horseshoe got her?

Peggy lay on her back, staring at the ceiling. She heard her parents go into their bedroom and close the door. "Luck, good or bad, is not to be trifled with," Granny had said. If she didn't know that before, she certainly knew it now.

Peggy threw back the covers, got out of bed, and switched on the light. She found her jeans under her bed. She pulled out the silver chain with the Cornish Piskie charm from the pocket and slipped it into the pocket of her pajama top. When she got back into bed, she felt better.

Chapter Seven

A Little Bit of Lipstick

Peggy stared at the clothes hanging in her wardrobe. She had absolutely nothing to wear. Reluctantly she pulled out her Sunday dress. It was a pale blue cotton dress with a white daisy pattern. She had thought that this dress was perfect when she had chosen it last year. Now she didn't know why she had chosen it. It didn't hang right anymore and it definitely made her knees look bony.

That was a fun day though, she mused. She had enjoyed riding the train to Plymouth for their annual shopping trip, chatting to her mother about what they would buy. There were plenty of shops in Penzance, but every summer they took the train to Plymouth, in Devon, where there were many more shops and more bargains to be had. It was a real adventure. Her mother had been as excited as she was. They cheered when they crossed the River Tamar. Her mother's father had been born in Devon and after their shopping trip, they went to Budleigh Salterton on a long bus ride. They stayed with relatives for the weekend and Peggy loved getting together with family she barely knew. They always made a fuss of her and claimed she looked just like her grandfather. She had been really close with her mother last year. Mum had changed. She wasn't fun to be with any more. Peggy had asked her when they were going this year – just to have something really fun to look forward to, but her mother had said she didn't know, and worse, she didn't care.

In the bathroom, Peggy brushed her hair. It needed a trim. To try to please her mother, Peggy braided her hair into two pigtails. She hunted in the drawer by the sink and found two blue ribbons that matched her dress. Grimacing, she tied the ribbons into bows on the end of her pigtails.

Peggy leaned closer to the mirror to examine her pimples and gasped. There were three of them now. She would need some lotion or something to put on them to stop them spreading all over her face. She would have to ask Mum about it. Her mother's eyes, blue with green specks, looked back at her in the mirror. She wished her eyes were a clear blue like her father's. She'd probably got her bony knees from him instead.

"Peggy?" she heard her mother call.

Peggy left the bathroom and ran downstairs. "Well now, don't you look a treat," her father said warmly. "You are more like your mother every day."

Peggy slid into her seat at the breakfast table. Boiled eggs. She hated boiled eggs. Her mother handed Peggy some toast and a jar of jam. "Thanks, Mum," Peggy said.

She helped her mother clear the table. They left the dishes in the scullery sink. Her mother went upstairs to finish getting ready for church. Her father went to the stone plot where he parked his old green van. Peggy looked out of the scullery window. Old Tom was grazing in the field. Sometimes Peggy rode Old Tom bareback around the field. He stood by the fence patiently while she climbed up and slid onto his back. With a few gentle kicks, Peggy could get him to trot for a few yards, but he always slowed down and brought her back to the fence. The farmer who owned Old Tom had told Peggy that she could ride him, but not too often. Old Tom deserved his rest and was out to pasture. Peggy opened the kitchen window. "Hello, Old Tom," she called. He ambled over, looking for his usual treat. Peggy often gave him a piece of her apple. "Later," she promised.

As she closed the window, she saw her mother's compact on the window ledge. Peggy picked it up and opened it. She dabbed some powder on her forehead to help to cover her pimples and powdered her nose and cheeks. She was pleased with how that looked. Her mother's lipstick was also on the window ledge beside her father's shaving mirror. Peggy pulled off the top. The lipstick was an orange-red color. She added color to her lips. There was no doubt about it, she decided. Makeup made her look prettier, although she doubted her mother would agree with her. "A little bit of lipstick, powder 'n' paint makes a girl look what she ain't," she chanted and giggled. She regretted putting her hair into pigtails. They made her look younger.

Peggy took one last look in the mirror and left the cottage to go to the stone plot. She climbed into the front seat of the van, careful to avoid the front seat spring. Sometimes the spring leaped out and attacked her, no matter how well her father pushed it back into the upholstery and taped it down.

The Parish church was full as usual, but the Tregarths found their favorite seats unoccupied because everybody knew where everyone else sat. Jimmy Wallace was sitting in the back row of the choir box. He used to sit in the front row, but a few months earlier he had sung a solo, and his voice had cracked on all of the high notes. Peggy had tried to be loyal and not join in on all the giggles at his performance, but it was funny.

Jimmy threw something at John Davis, sitting three rows in front of him. The younger boy whipped around and stuck his tongue out. Jimmy studied his prayer book with a serious face. The choirmaster said something in a low voice, and John turned scarlet to the tips of his ears, which stuck out like handles on a teacup. Peggy grinned.

Jill Willis was sitting in the pew in front of the Tregarths. Peggy tapped her on the shoulder. Jill turned around. "Hello," she said. "Did you ..."

"Ssh," Jill's mother said.

When the vicar gave his sermon, he told everyone that hard times would make them better and stronger people. They were all God's children, he said, and no adversities should turn brother against brother. Peggy thought he must have heard about Trevor Vernon wanting to fight the Scots because he kept repeating that the Scots were God's children as each and every one of the congregation was a child of God. She turned around to see if Mr. Vernon would object, but he was nodding and smiling as though he agreed with everything the vicar said.

The Sunday school class joined them just as they were about to sing the collection hymn. There was a lot of shuffling about while the younger children found their families, and settled down for the end of the service and the announcements. The choir stood up to sing. Jimmy was so tall he stood out even in the back row, a full head above some of the other boys. Most of them looked like geeks in their black choir cassocks, but Jimmy looked cool. Peggy loved the way his fair hair curled around his ears. His bright blue eyes met her eyes at the exact moment she was admiring him. Peggy quickly looked down, feeling her cheeks burn. When she looked up again, he was still watching her. He grinned. Then he winked at her. Feeling flustered, Peggy opened her hymnal and began to sing.

At the end of the service, people greeted each other outside and chatted. "It's all very well for a man of the cloth to preach peace," Peggy heard Trevor Vernon say to Theo Willis. "That don't help us none, does it?"

"It is what it is," Theo Willis said, turning away. He started a conversation with Mr. and Mrs. Rogers. They owned a dairy farm and didn't fish.

"Make them pay for taking what's not theirs to take," Trevor Vernon said to Joe Chapple, who was standing next to him. "It's our bloody fish!" Peggy wondered why he cared so much about the fish. He had a pig farm, not a fishing boat. Peggy always thought Mr. Vernon looked like a ferret. He was thin, had a pointed nose, scraggly black hair, and tiny dark eyes.

Jill ran up to Peggy. "Did you hear the news?" she asked. "We're leaving. Dad had a job offer on one of the Hull trawlers. We're going to live with my Aunt Jessie. Jill's brown eyes were filled with tears.

Peggy gasped. "But Jill, trawlers are the enemy! They're stealing our fish."

Jill pushed a stray fair hair from her face. "I know," she whispered. "It's because of them we have to sell our boat."

"Sorry," Peggy said, mentally kicking herself. "I'm sorry you're leaving, Jill. I thought we could ride the bus together next year."

"Me, too," Jill said sadly. Her mother called her and she ran over to join her.

Peggy looked for her parents. Her mother was talking to Mrs. Vernon who seemed to be arguing with her about something. Peggy watched them for a moment. Mrs. Vernon looked just like one of her pigs, she decided. She was short and fat, with a flat nose and sparse, white hair. Her father was talking to the vicar. They were smiling at each other and they shook hands.

"Nice chap," her father said, coming over to where Peggy stood. He put his arm around her shoulders.

Her mother hurried over to join them. "That woman drives me batty," she said and led the way to the van. Peggy looked back at the church to see if she could see Jimmy. He wasn't there. Maybe he was changing out of his cassock.

"I'll hear an explanation, Peggy, if you please," her mother said in a voice of steel.

Peggy climbed into the van. Her heart jumped. Had her mother found out about the horseshoe? "What about, Mum?" she asked in what she hoped was a casual tone.

"My makeup on your face, Peggy Tregarth!"

Was that all? Relieved, Peggy said, "It's just a little bit, Mum. My face was all shiny from the wind. I wanted to look nice for church. You always say we should look our best for church."

"You're too young for makeup," her mother answered sharply. "You're just a child, Peggy. Twelve years old is too young to be painting your face."

"But I'm on the way to being thirteen, Mum. Everybody wears makeup at thirteen," Peggy said.

"Everybody can do what they like," her mother said coldly. "You are not everybody. You'll scrub your face clean when we get home. Not another word out of your mouth, Peggy," her mother warned as Peggy continued to protest.

Peggy wriggled about on her seat. "Ouch!" she cried when the sneaky spring sprang and smacked her on her bare thigh. "I wish you would get that mended, Dad."

Her father laughed. "It's a rascal. No matter how many times I put it back, it jumps right out again. Sorry, love."

Peggy glared at him and slumped in her seat.

Her father pulled into a gravel area to let the bus going the other way pass them. The narrow country roads were not wide enough for two cars to pass without one of them pulling over. "After we have a bite to eat, I'm going out to the pots," he announced.

"Bill, it's a Sunday," her mother protested.

"I don't think the Lord will object if I go and see if there's a lobster for our tea tonight," he said cheerfully. "I think we could all do with a bit of change and every shellfish I've caught has had to go to market the way things are."

"Can I go?" Peggy asked him.

"Just what I had in mind." Her father turned and grinned at her.

"But, Dad, did you forget? *The Sunrise* is at the boat-yard in Newlyn."

"I had a word with Joe Chapple at church this morning, Peggy." He pulled into the stone plot. "Joe told me the boat-yard got to *The Sunrise* yesterday afternoon. She's ready and waiting for us in Newlyn Harbor."

"Brilliant," Peggy cried and jumped out of the van. She raced up the lane ahead of her parents to change her clothes. In the bathroom, she used a flannel to wipe the makeup from her face. She was about to slide the banister back down to the kitchen, when she changed her mind. Peggy ran back into her bedroom and grabbed her pajama top. She took the silver chain with the charm out of her pajama top pocket and slipped it into the pocket of her jeans.

Peggy had just finished putting the last dish away from

the lunch dishes when her father put on his heavy, water-proof sea coat. "Time to go," he said. Peggy reached for her jacket, hanging on a peg beside the door. Her stomach felt queasy again as she watched her father tap the horseshoe for luck. Peggy immediately slipped her hand into her jeans pocket. Her fingers touched the Piskie charm.

It was five o'clock when Peggy burst triumphantly into the cottage. "We got a lobster for tea, Mum," she cried happily. "Dad let me take the boat all the way from Newlyn to the pots, and he even let me take it into the cove. I could feel the currents pulling us by the rocks, but I'm learning the waters, right Dad?"

Her father hung up his coat. "I was proud of the way she handled the boat, Jean," he said. "A true Tregarth is what she is."

Grinning from ear to ear, Peggy ran upstairs to change her jumper. The sleeves were soaked in salt water. The grin left her face when she overheard her parents' conversation. "I know from the look on your face, Jean, that we should be selling that lobster," her father said. "I just wanted to get us something special for tea. I miss the roast."

"Well, I've not paid the butcher in over a month, Bill. I didn't feel right about ordering any meat 'til we'd paid for what's been eaten!" her mother snapped.

"I know, I know," her father said, his voice sounding tired.

Peggy pulled a green jumper from the second drawer in her chest of drawers. For just a little while she had forgotten everything. Some of the joy of the day left her. Mum couldn't pay the butcher? Things must be bad. She closed the drawer, and ran to the bathroom to wash for tea.

When her mother put the large, blue-black speckled

lobster into a large saucepan of water, Peggy ran out of the scullery. Her mother had told her on several occasions that the lobster didn't feel like a person would, but Peggy couldn't bear to hear him scraping his claws at the sides of the pan. Every time they had lobster, Peggy wanted to yank the lid off the pan and rescue the poor thing. It was a pity that you had to cook lobsters alive, she thought sadly.

Peggy came back into the scullery when it was time to remove the meat from the lobster's shell. It was now a bright orange color and her mother said he was a beauty. "Can I crack the claws?" she asked.

Her mother smiled. "Then you can pinch a bit before we eat?"

Peggy picked up the small hammer. She stared at it. She saw herself hammering the nails into the door to make sure that the horseshoe looked the same as it had before it had fallen off. Abruptly she left the scullery. "Um, I have to go to the bathroom," she muttered, and ran back to her room.

Surprising both her parents, Peggy went straight to her bedroom after the dinner dishes were done. They had asked her to join them in a game of scrabble. Peggy normally loved to play scrabble, but she wanted to be alone to work on her plan. It was harder than she had imagined it would be, and as one thought came into her mind, another replaced it. She had to get it exactly right.

Later that night, Peggy heard someone crying. The sobs were muffled. Peggy opened her bedroom door. She crept onto the landing between her room and her parents' room. It was her mother who was crying. Peggy heard her say, between sobs, "Bill, you love that boat. Selling it would be like selling a part of yourself."

Her father's voice was low. Peggy could hardly hear what he was saying, but she understood the gist of it. Somebody had made her father an offer for *The Sunrise*.

Peggy crept back to her bedroom. If she dreamed her nightmare tonight, she would tell that horseshoe that it was not going to win. She would shout that it was not going to win right into its horrible, evil face!

Peggy turned on the light, and wrote an additional item in her notebook. It was item number six. She got back into bed and slept a dreamless sleep.

Chapter Eight

The Gift

Peggy was sitting on the floor with her china horse bank when her mother came into her room. "Spring cleaning time," she announced. "It's a fine morning. We are going to scour this house from top to bottom."

"Today?" Peggy asked, dismayed.

"Today," her mother replied. She swept Peggy's bed-clothes onto the floor. "You can start with the bedding. There's a crisp breeze blowing and it's a good day to get the bedding washed and dried."

When her mother had left the room, Peggy scrambled over to her pajama top that was tangled in one of her sheets. She removed the silver chain and charm, and slipped it once again into her jeans pocket. Carefully she replaced the horse bank on the top of her chest of drawers. Item number one on her plan list was complete.

"I have to go to Treen to the shop, Peggy," her mother called up the stairs. "You start on the wash and I'll be home to help you."

"Right, Mum," Peggy called back. She stepped over to the window and watched her mother walk down the path. When she was sure her mother was gone, Peggy ran down the stairs to the sitting room and picked up the local telephone book. It was beside the black telephone on a small table at one end of the sofa. When she had located the number she wanted, Peggy picked up the telephone. She was about to dial the number when she realized that there was no dial tone. She jiggled the handset button. Still no dial tone. Irritated, Peggy replaced the receiver. Peggy grabbed her jacket from the peg by the front door and left the cottage.

It was time to complete item number two on her list, and she had worked out just where she could buy what she needed. She had wanted to call first, but the telephone was out of order. It won't take long, she told herself. She would be back before her mother even knew she had left the cottage.

It would be quicker if she still had her bike. She could take the roads. Three weeks earlier, she had put her bicycle down in the road for just a moment to rescue a baby magpie that had fallen from its nest. A Massey-Ferguson tractor came out of a side road and had run over her bike as though it was a twig on the road. Peggy had walked home in tears. Her father had driven the van to pick it up and had told her it was a total loss. The wheels were buckled, the gears twisted, and the handlebars were badly bent. Peggy consoled herself by thinking that the tractor's huge wheels would have crushed the baby magpie if she had not stopped to rescue it. That would have been much worse than losing her bike.

She had to cross their daffodil fields to reach her destination. The whole field was full of wilting King Alfreds. The next field was just like the first field. "It's so unfair," she muttered. Peggy ran through the fields, eager to escape the devastation all around her. She crossed the road to the other side of the valley, and almost stepped on a hedgehog that was lying on its back. Small legs waved in the air helplessly. "You can't turn yourself, can you?" she said sympathetically. With the toe of her shoe, Peggy gently flipped the prickly animal over. Immediately it huddled into a little ball with spikes.

When Peggy arrived at the dairy farm, she found Mrs. Rogers feeding the chickens in the yard. She was a heavyset, middle-aged woman with tightly curled brown hair. Her small, blue eyes sparkled with interest when Peggy came towards her, but she continued to scatter grain for the young chicks. Peggy laughed as she watched them toddle about on unsteady legs, cheeping. She picked up a fluffy yellow baby and gently stroked it with one finger on its tiny head. "They're so sweet," she said.

"I like them that age, too," Mrs. Rogers said fondly. "I never get tired of the chicks, but I lose some if I'm not careful. There's a smart fox about."

Peggy gulped. Was it her fox? She cleared her throat. "Do you have any cream for sale, Mrs. Rogers?"

"Clotted cream, you mean?" Mrs. Rogers asked.

"Yes, please," Peggy answered.

"We don't make it, nor sell it."

"Oh," Peggy said. "I didn't know. I mean I thought a dairy farm would have cream and I could buy some."

Mrs. Rogers smiled. "My mother used to make clotted cream. She would set a saucepan on the stove filled with water and put a big china bowl filled with fresh milk in the center of the pan. The heat was on low, and the cream came to the top and formed a crust. There was nothing better than my mum's clotted cream." Mrs. Rogers tipped the rest of the chicken feed onto the ground and tucked the pan under her arm. "Of course health regulations changed everything you know. Pasteurization, Peggy."

Disappointed, Peggy put the chick back down into the

yard. Cheeping, it ran to join the others. "Do you know where I could buy some cream, Mrs. Rogers?"

"You can order it from the milkman, Peggy. Sometimes you can get it in the village shop at St. Buryan, but they don't always have it. Of course, you can always get it in Penzance." She eyed Peggy thoughtfully. "Did you ask your mother, Peggy? She'd know the cream she likes the best."

"I didn't ask Mum," Peggy answered. "It's for a surprise," she added quickly.

"Making something special?" Mrs. Rogers smiled warmly at her. "My boys wouldn't think of surprising me in a month of Sundays," she said.

Peggy turned to leave. "Thank you for your help, Mrs. Rogers," she said.

"Lovely to see you, Peggy. Drop by any time, dear. Come and see Prince next time. He's out with my husband, tending to the cows."

Peggy walked away slowly. She needed to buy the cream today. There was a bus to Penzance at around eleven. Without thinking, she glanced at her wrist. No watch. She had lost it over a week ago when she was climbing the cliffs. That's where she thought she had lost it. She wasn't really sure.

The problem is, she thought, is that Mum will see me. Sometimes she stays for a chat when she goes to Treen, and that's the only place I can catch the bus. If I get off at St. Buryan and the village shop doesn't have any, I would have to wait forever for another bus to Penzance. Lost in thought, and with decisions to make, Peggy climbed over a gate to cross a field without checking it first. Peggy was half-way across the field when she saw him. Grazing behind a large oak tree, not more than five yards from her, was an enormous black bull.

Peggy froze. She stared at the bull in horror. Stay calm, she ordered herself, as she felt her face tighten, and her heart jump in her chest. She looked down at her clothes. She was wearing blue jeans, a green sweater, and a blue jacket. At least she was not wearing red. With trembling fingers, Peggy zipped up her jacket so that it would not flap as she ran.

Should she go forward or should she go backwards? Tentatively, she took a step backwards, watching the bull. He looked up. He looked right at her. Peggy couldn't breath. The bull pawed at the ground. He wouldn't permit any intruders in his field and now he knew she was there! "Forward," she gasped. She had to run to the gate on the other side of the field, which looked miles away.

What was the matter with her legs? They felt like they were made of jelly. They wouldn't work! The bull glared at her motionless form. He lowered his head and began to graze again. It was now or never, Peggy decided. Forcing her legs to respond, Peggy sprinted for the gate. She heard the bull snort. There were terrifying sounds of his hoofs pounding the turf behind her. Peggy knew she would never make it to the gate in time.

Someone vaulted over the gate ahead of her, passed her, shouting, waving his arms. Peggy stumbled, recovered, and raced to the gate. She scrambled over it, gasping for breath. She whirled around to see what was happening. Who was that?

Peggy saw a familiar figure zigzagging across the field, the bull in hot pursuit. It was Jimmy! He was running towards the other gate. The bull was close to him, his head down, and his intent serious. Peggy could hardly stand it. "Run, Jimmy, run," she screamed. When Jimmy threw himself over the heavy wooden slats, the bull crashed into the gate. He charged it again before trotting away, swishing his black stringy tail.

Peggy stood on the gate, trying to see Jimmy. Was he all right? She eyed the bull suspiciously, but he was back to grazing on the far side of the field. Minutes passed. There was no sign of Jimmy. Peggy kept her eyes fixed on the other gate. He had to be all right. Her hands were trembling as she gripped the slats. Realization flooded in. Jimmy Wallace had saved her life.

"Don't you know any better than to go wandering about in a field owned by a bull?" Jimmy's voice was behind her. Peggy stepped down from the gate and turned around. "Jimmy," she cried and burst into tears.

Chapter Nine

Tit for Tat

Peggy and Jimmy sat on a stone wall amidst the primroses and wild daffodils to recover from their shared experience. Jimmy was nice about her tears. He said his sister used to cry every time she was scared, too. He brushed off her thanks and refused to entertain the idea that he had saved her life. "You would have made it, Peggy," he said with a grin. "I was looking for some excitement, that's all."

They sat for a while, not saying anything. Peggy felt comfortable with Jimmy. She didn't feel shy any more. He was the nicest boy she had ever met and even though he had denied it, he had definitely saved her life. "What are you doing over this way?" Jimmy asked.

"I needed to get some clotted cream," Peggy answered without thinking.

Jimmy laughed. "For the Piskies?"

Peggy looked at him in astonishment. Was he a psychic, too? She was about to lie to him, but changed her mind. "Mrs. Rogers doesn't sell clotted cream. I'll have to go to St. Buryan, or into Penzance."

"Oh, I don't think you have to do that, Peggy," Jimmy answered casually. "We've got it up at the house. Mum is baking apple pies as we speak, so I know she must have ordered some from the milkman. You can't eat apple pie without cream."

"I couldn't take your cream, Jimmy. That wouldn't be right," Peggy answered.

"Why not? It would save you a trip on that slow bus," Jimmy said. They both laughed at the same time.

Peggy thought about Treen, her mother, and all the complications of going into Penzance if the village shop didn't have any cream. "If you're positive it would be okay with your mother," she said finally

They walked across three fields. Jimmy climbed up on all of the gates, pretending to scout for bulls. Peggy laughed every time. When they were back on the road, Peggy asked, "How do you know about cream and Piskies, Jimmy?"

"My sister, Sarah. She was mad about the Piskies. She's at the University now so this is way back. I think she was about thirteen and I was eight."

"Did she make a wish, Jimmy?" Peggy asked.

"That's what I was thinking about when you said you needed clotted cream. I've been feeling guilty about something I did back then," Jimmy said seriously.

"What happened?" Peggy asked, now very curious.

"Sarah wanted something badly. She was talking to her friend Jane about it on the phone and I was listening in. Anyways, she told Jane that she was going to wish for what she wanted. She was going to ask the Piskies."

"What was it she wanted?" Peggy asked, leaning back into a primrose-covered hedgerow to let a car pass by.

"I don't know. She wouldn't even tell Jane because she said it wouldn't come true if she told anybody. She just said she was going to make a wish. It's up this way," Jimmy said, leading the way to his house.

"Are your parents at home?" Peggy asked eyeing his house with apprehension.

"Mum is. Dad's at work. He's a doctor at *West Cornwall.*" He bent down to pick a newspaper off his driveway. "Mum'll be happy to meet you. She likes to meet my friends."

Peggy felt warm inside. He had called her his friend. Jimmy pointed to a beautiful pink rhododendron bush on the left of the driveway. "That's where Sarah put the cream for the Piskies. She said they probably lived in the blooms." It was a lovely bush. Peggy walked over to it. Her mother had one just like it in her garden, except that the blooms on her mother's bush were a darker pink. "Sarah put the cream on a silver dish under the bush," Jimmy said, joining her. "It was really late at night, but I heard her sneak out of the house and I followed her."

"What happened?" Peggy asked, totally absorbed in his story.

"Well, that's the thing. I got up really early the next day, before the sun was up. I wanted to see the Piskies, too. I hid behind that gardening shed." He pointed to a small white-washed building to the left of the house. "I saw both our cats over by the bush. I knew what they were doing. Our cats are mad for cream. I ran over one time and shooed them away, but I was afraid Sarah would see me and the cats came back."

"But Jimmy, didn't Sarah know that the cats would get at the cream? My cat, Nimbob, would track it down wherever it was." Peggy said.

Jimmy kicked at the mud by the bush. "That's the thing, Peggy. I let the cats out when I went out. Sarah had locked them in for the night. I was the one who let them out."

Peggy looked away so that Jimmy couldn't see the expression of dismay on her face. She cleared her throat.

"What happened then?" she asked.

"Sarah came out of the front door. The cats were gone by then. They had polished off the lot. She ran over to the bush and picked up the empty silver dish. I could see she was excited. She was jumping up and down, laughing. Then she did this little dance around the bush. She sang something, but I couldn't hear the words. I guess she was making a wish."

"Did you see any Piskies?" Peggy asked.

"I hoped I would, but all I saw was Sarah, dancing about in her best dress, singing," Jimmy said, swatting an insect from his face.

"Do you know if her wish came true?" Peggy asked.

"The Piskies didn't take the cream, did they? The cats did. Sarah was very upset with the Piskies. She had a thing at the time about trust. If she found out someone had told her a lie, she never spoke to them again. Sarah said that the Piskies had betrayed her trust because they had tricked her. They had fooled her by eating all the cream and then they didn't grant her wish. Of course, she didn't tell me about it, but I heard her on the phone talking to Jane. She said that she felt like a fool, dancing and singing, believing in them. I remember it like it was yesterday, Peggy."

"You didn't tell her, Jimmy?" Peggy asked, feeling sorry for Sarah, even though she didn't even know her.

"I was afraid to tell her," Jimmy said with a short laugh. "In fact, you are the first person I've ever told the story to."

Peggy nodded slowly. She understood. It was hard to tell someone you looked up to that you had made a really bad mistake. "I think you should tell her, Jimmy," she said finally. "She may be mad at you at first, but you should tell her anyway. Don't you think that she would be glad to know that the Piskies hadn't tricked her?"

Jimmy frowned. "You mean I should tell her that it was me that tricked her, not the Piskies?"

Peggy laughed. "No! You didn't trick her, Jimmy. The cats did. All you did was let the cats out. Besides, I think that the Piskies would have taken the cream in the night if they had been there, don't you think? Before you let the cats out?"

Jimmy nodded. "Could be," he said thoughtfully. "Come on then, we'll get you that cream."

Jimmy led the way to the back of the house. It was a large granite house with white painted window trim. There were pretty blue flowered curtains at all the windows. The front garden was filled with camellias, daffodils, Christmas roses, and red and yellow tulips. It was beautiful Peggy thought with admiration. Jimmy's parents had planted a large vegetable garden in the back that was flourishing. "That's Mum's pride and joy," he said, pointing to the vegetables.

Mrs. Wallace looked up with a smile when they entered the kitchen. She was an attractive woman with dark brown hair, graying at the temples. When she smiled, Peggy could see a likeness to Jimmy. They had the same eyes. There were two apple pies on the counter, with golden brown crusts. She was busy on a third, slicing the peeled apples into the pie pan. "I thought two would be enough, Jimmy, but your father just called and said he had invited two more for dinner tonight." Mrs. Wallace put the apple she was slicing down and wiped her hands on a dishtowel. "And who's this?" she asked, looking at Peggy.

"This is Peggy Tregarth, Mum," Jimmy said. "She goes to *Trinity* and rides the same bus as me every day."

Mrs. Wallace smiled warmly at Peggy. "Oh, yes, dear, I think I've seen you before with your parents at church. It's nice to meet you," she said.

Peggy responded to her warm tone. "Thank you," she said. "It's nice to meet you, too."

"Mum, I think I saw a rabbit out in your vegetable garden. He's after your purple-sprouting broccoli. There could be two," Jimmy said.

"What? Rabbits?" Mrs. Wallace cried and hurried past them into the back garden.

Jimmy crossed the kitchen and opened the refrigerator. He removed a small cardboard container of clotted cream from one of the shelves and closed the door. Casually, he slipped it into his jacket pocket. "Jimmy, your mother needs that for her guests tonight," Peggy protested.

"There's a really big container in there, Peggy. She won't need this one." He patted his pocket. "Let's go."

"I can't take it, Jimmy. I have to pay for it," Peggy said. She put her right hand into her jeans' pocket and pulled out some coins.

Mrs. Wallace bustled back into the kitchen. "They're all gone now," she said with satisfaction. "You were right, Jimmy, except I chased off three."

Peggy's eyes widened. She hadn't seen any, but then, she wasn't looking for rabbits. Jimmy made a move to the door. Peggy stood still. Summoning her courage, she said, "Mrs. Wallace, do you have enough cream to go with those lovely pies?"

"Yes, dear." Mrs. Wallace opened the refrigerator. "I have a big container of clotted cream and a bottle of the thin cream for those who prefer it." Mrs. Wallace looked at Peggy curiously. "Worry about things like that, do you?"

Peggy blushed. "Jimmy showed me a small container."

Mrs. Wallace laughed. "I always order a small one for my babies. Jimmy takes care of them. They get one teaspoon a day for a treat."

Outside, Peggy turned on Jimmy and said, fiercely, "You can't give me cream that you are supposed to give to your mother's babies."

Jimmy laughed. "Tit for tat," he said. "The small container of cream is for the cats. Mum always calls them her babies. Look, Peggy, they stole cream once, meant for the Piskies, so it's a fair trade." He took the cream from his pocket and handed it to her. "I owe this to the Piskies, Peg." Peggy considered what he had said. It made total sense. Peggy slipped it into her jacket pocket.

Jimmy walked Peggy back down the driveway. His mother called after them. "Jimmy, did you get the eggs from Mrs. Rogers?"

"Going now, Mum," he called back.

"Thanks, Jimmy," Peggy said. " Thanks for saving me, from the bull, the cream and everything. I have to run now or Mum is going to have a fit."

"Peggy, your dad has a fishing boat doesn't he?" Jimmy asked.

Peggy nodded. "*The Sunrise*," she said.

"Do you think he would take me out in it sometime? I want to see if there are any caves on the other side of the cliffs."

"I love caves," Peggy said enthusiastically. "I'll ask him. He's teaching me to handle the boat, so maybe I could take you out myself."

"Brilliant," Jimmy said. "See you."

"See you," Peggy answered.

Chapter Ten

Grounded

Peggy ran home as fast as she could. She knew her mother would be back at the cottage and looking for her. She would help her all day and work on her plan that night. First, she would complete item number three and then it would be time for item number four. She slipped her hand into her jacket pocket and felt the small container of cream.

When Peggy ran up the path to Chyoak, she saw her mother hanging wash on the line. "Hello, Mum," she said. "Sorry, I had to do something. I had to go out, but I can help you now."

Her mother turned to face her. "Go to your room, Peggy," she said coldly.

"To bring the bedding down?" Peggy asked.

"No," her mother snapped. "Go there and stay there. I can't stand the sight of you."

Peggy flinched. "I want to help you, Mum," she said earnestly. "Honest I do."

"I said go to your room, Peggy. I mean it. I'm too angry to deal with you right now." Her mother pulled a large sheet out of the laundry basket. It caught on the handle of the basket. When she yanked it free, the basket tipped up, and all of the clean wet clothes fell onto the ground and into the mud. Peggy darted forward to help. Her mother stopped her. "Go to your room!" she shouted.

With a muffled sob, Peggy ran into the cottage and up to her bedroom. It was as she had left it. Her bedclothes were still on the floor, mixed up with her dirty clothes. Her backpack was also on the floor, the books, pencils, and pens scattered. Peggy sat on the mattress. Mum had never been this angry with her before. She wiped away the tears running down her cheeks. It must be that horseshoe's fault, she decided. Everything was hateful ever since she had knocked it down. Peggy took a deep breath. "You are not going to win," she said in a firm voice. "You may be winning right now, but not for long!"

Peggy got up and started to tidy her room. First, she remade the bed with clean sheets. Then she took the soiled sheets and clothes to the hamper in the bathroom. She washed her face and hands, and brushed her hair. Feeling better and full of resolve, Peggy came back into her bedroom. She sat on the bed, her notepad and pen in her hand, and decided to work on item number four. She put a check mark on item number one and then on item number two. She smiled as she checked off item number two. Jimmy was special. There was no doubt about it. He had saved her from that horrible bull and then he had given her the cream. She thought about the story he had told her about his sister, Sarah, and wondered what Sarah had wished for. From what Jimmy had said, the Piskies hadn't granted her wish, but the Piskies had not eaten the cream. The cats ate it.

Peggy jumped up. The cream! It would go sour in her pocket. Peggy took it out of her jacket pocket and went to the window. Her mother was not at the clothesline. She must have taken the wash back in to redo. Peggy opened her window and placed the carton of clotted cream on the ledge outside. It was getting colder and the cool breezes would keep it fresh for a while at least.

Taking the silver chain and the Piskie charm out of her pocket, she laid it beside her on the bed. She was sure it would inspire her. Item number four on the list was to work out exactly what she should say when she took the gift to the Piskies. She had been trying out different phrases in her mind, but none of them seemed right. It had to be perfect. Item number four had two parts: A and B. Part A was what she should say when she took the gift and part B was what she would say when she made the wish. Of course, if the Piskies didn't take the cream, she wouldn't need part B of number four. Peggy pushed that thought from her mind. She had to stay positive.

Granny had chanted a rhyme that day on the cliffs. "The gift must be given before the clock strikes eleven," Peggy murmured. "The wish must be made by half-past seven." Granny's rhyme had sounded magical. Maybe the best way to talk to the Piskies was in rhyme. Peggy liked making up poems, but the two poems she had to make up today were the most important poems she would ever write.

She got up and turned on the light. It was getting dark outside even though it was early. Uneasily she thought of what this meant. A storm was on the way, tonight of all nights.

Peggy heard her father's voice downstairs. He had to come in from sea because of the bad weather, she thought. Her father always said the sea told him about a storm on its way before the sky turned dark. Peggy opened her door. Her father was laughing. "What are you going to do with that lot?" he said. "It'll have to wait until morning now."

"I said I was going to do it and I always do what I say I'll do," her mother said. Then she started to laugh, too. "I'll leave it in the bathtub until morning," she said.

Peggy felt left out. They were downstairs, joking about the wet laundry and laughing, and she was upstairs, all by herself.

"Where's Peg?" her father asked. "I want her home with the storm coming in."

"She's home. I sent her to her room. I don't know what to do with her. She's so irresponsible, Bill. And she disobeys me constantly. She just doesn't care about anything but herself. I'm at my wits end with that child."

Peggy swallowed passed the lump in her throat. She did, too, care. She was trying as hard as she could to help.

"Don't be so hard on her, Jean," her father said. "She's just a little girl with a lot to learn. Let's put the kettle on and have a nice cup of tea."

Peggy closed her door. She didn't want to hear any more insults. She wanted to run downstairs and defend herself, but she couldn't do that. She couldn't tell them how much she cared, or how hard she was trying, because it was a secret. "Tell that wish to a living soul, sure as death it will fall afoul," Granny had said.

Peggy read the rhymes she had worked on. She knew them by heart and they sounded good, but were they good enough? Thunder rolled in the distance. Peggy looked out of the window. The sky was dark, but it hadn't started to rain yet. She went over to the drawer in her bedside table and found her torch. She turned it on. It worked. Good, she thought. It's the only light I'll have tonight.

"Peggy?" her mother called.

Peggy opened her door and stood at the top of the stairs.

"Yes, Mum?"

"You can come down for tea," her mother said.

Peggy was surprised that it was that late. She walked down the stairs slowly. Her mother had made a cheese and potato pie for tea. "You missed lunch, so I thought you would be hungry," her mother said.

Peggy nodded. "Thank you," she said quietly. It was hard to forget the things her mother had said to her and about her. Peggy felt like a stranger at her own kitchen table.

Her father didn't seem to be aware that anything was wrong between his wife and his daughter. He talked about how heavy the swell had become and that all of the boats had come in early because of it.

Peggy helped to clear the table, but did not help with the dishes. She felt too uncomfortable to be in the scullery with her mother. She went back to her room, leaving her father reading the paper and her mother washing the dishes.

When the storm began, it was fierce. Rain lashed at the windows and the wind roared around the little cottage as though it was a live thing on a rampage. Peggy had rescued her cream as soon as the rain began. The container was cold. The cream had stayed fresh.

What should she serve the cream in? Jimmy had said that Sarah had used a silver dish. Mum had silver dishes, but they were tarnished. They only used them on very special occasions. It was Peggy's job to polish them at Christmas. Then she remembered her grandmother's bone china set that her mother kept in the top cupboard of the kitchen dresser She could use a bone china saucer with a gold trim and pretty blue flowers all around the edge. Peggy smiled, pleased with her idea. Maybe she could leave just a teaspoon of cream in the carton for Nimbob. He was so partial to cream.

Where was Nimbob? She hadn't seen him when she went down for tea. Where was he?

Chapter Eleven

Lost in the Storm

Peggy ran downstairs and called Nimbob. He didn't run to her as he always did. He couldn't be out in this lashing rain, could he? Nimbob was scared of thunder. He always hid under her bed when a storm swept the valley. He wasn't in her room. She would have seen him. Nevertheless, Peggy ran back upstairs and looked under her bed. He wasn't there. She went into her parents' room and looked under their bed in case Nimbob had come upstairs and found her door closed. A quick look in the bathroom confirmed he wasn't upstairs.

The sitting room door was closed. Relieved, Peggy decided that he must be in there with her parents. He liked to curl up on her father's lap. She knocked on the door. "Excuse me," she said. "Is Nimbob in here?"

Her mother was sitting on the sofa with her father. There was a pile of envelopes on the coffee table in front of them. They looked like bills. Her mother looked up from a letter she was reading. "He's not in here with us, Peggy. You should look under your bed. That's where he goes when there's a storm."

"I know. I looked. He's not there," Peggy answered.

"Well, he's not here either, Peggy," her father said.

"Go along now."

Dismissed, Peggy closed the sitting room door. She looked in the window seat by the kitchen window and ran into the scullery, calling his name. When she opened the back door she expected to see his wet, bedraggled little body huddled outside, but only the rain, wind, and darkness was outside the door.

Peggy ran back to her room to get her torch. As she ran back downstairs she glared up at Tregarth's Good Luck. "He's just a little cat," she hissed. "Don't you dare hurt him again!"

The front door fought her as she tried to open it. The fierce wind was pressing it into the latch and it wouldn't open. Peggy tugged on it until it burst open. Rain swept into the cottage. Her mother opened the sitting room door. "What on earth are you doing?" she cried, pushing the front door with both hands until it was closed. "Look at this mess!"

Peggy looked down at the floor. Water, mud, and green leaves were on the yellow linoleum floor. "Mum, I can't find Nimbob," she said, close to tears.

Her mother had gone out to the scullery to get the floor mop. "He's all right, Peggy," she said. "He's hiding somewhere until this storm is over. He'll be home in the morning. Go on up to bed. I don't have time for your nonsense tonight."

"It's not nonsense, Mum," Peggy answered crossly. "Nimbob is out there in this storm. He's scared and he's all alone."

"Don't think for one minute I will allow you to go out in this and look for that cat, Peggy," her mother said sternly.

Her father loomed in the doorway of the sitting room.

"You heard your mother, Peggy. Go on up to bed."

Peggy fled upstairs, so upset with both of them, she felt breathless. She opened her bedroom window. "Nimbob, here kitty, kitty," she called and shone her torch over the garden. The wind brought the rain into her bedroom, soaking the curtains and Peggy's sweater, as she leaned out, desperate to find her little cat.

Upset and worried, Peggy sat on her bed, fully dressed. She had spent a long time calling Nimbob and it was only when her torch went out that she gave up. She used a towel from the bathroom to mop up the mess the open window had caused. When she rummaged through all of her drawers, she couldn't find two new D batteries for the only light she would have tonight. There was a chance there might be some D's in the dresser drawer in the kitchen, but she had to wait for her parents to go to bed before she could even look.

When she finally heard her parents coming up the stairs, she glanced at the clock. It was almost ten. She only had an hour to meet the deadline. Quickly she jumped into the bed and pulled the covers up to her chin, but neither her father nor her mother opened her door. Her father took a long time in the bathroom. Peggy kept looking at the clock on her bedside table. "Hurry up, Dad," she muttered. Finally she heard her parents' bedroom door close.

Peggy waited a few more minutes and slipped out of bed. She stuffed her pillow under the covers so that her bed would look occupied. Peggy picked up the small container of cream and her torch, and tiptoed out of her room. The wooden floorboards creaked as she crept downstairs. If her parents heard the creaking boards, they would probably think they were a part of the storm, she decided.

It was dark in the kitchen, but Peggy was afraid to

switch on the kitchen light. Her parents' room was above the kitchen and if they did not have their curtains closed, they would see the light shining out into the garden. Peggy switched on the scullery light and returned to the dresser drawer. There was one new D battery. It was not as good as two, but her torch would probably work for a while. Peggy unscrewed the top of her torch, removed one of the dead batteries, and replaced it with the one from the kitchen drawer.

Quietly, she took a chair over to the kitchen dresser. She climbed on the chair and opened the top cupboard. Pleased, she saw that she had remembered correctly. Her grandmother's bone china tea set was there. She carefully removed one saucer from the stack and climbed down off the chair.

Her tan mackintosh and black Wellington boots were by the back door. As she buttoned up her raincoat and belted it tightly, she heard the wind howling outside. She had hoped the storm would have died down a little by now. It was windy on the cliffs even on sunny days. Peggy wrapped the china saucer in a clean, dry dishtowel and carefully put it into the pocket of her raincoat. She put the cream in the other side pocket. When she pulled the hood of her raincoat over her hair, she felt ready for the onslaught of the storm.

Peggy switched off the scullery light, picked up her torch, opened the back door, and went outside. It was time for item number four, part A. The wind grabbed her as though she was a new plaything. It threw her back against the cottage. Peggy fought against it, bent her head, ducked under the clotheslines, and waded through the puddles on the path towards the heifer field. "Nimby?" she called, shining her torch into hundreds of droplets of water. She listened for the sound of his voice in vain. "I'll find you, Nimbob," Peggy vowed. "When I get back, I'll find you."

Peggy climbed over the gate. Her rubber boots made sucking noises as she struggled to make progress in the thick, wet mud. Her raincoat was soaked through, clinging around her wet jeans. Her hood had blown off and the wind whipped her wet hair back into her face. She almost fell over the stile in the darkness. Peggy switched on her torch briefly. She had to save the battery for the cliffs ahead.

When the storm had first started, she had hoped it would not be a bad one. It was. Then she had hoped it would be over when she had to go to the cliffs. It wasn't. Now, as she struggled against it, she wondered if she should revise her plan. Item number three was location and Peggy had decided to take the gift to the Piskies at Logan Rock. Of course, that was before she knew there was going to be a storm. Even when she left the cottage, she hadn't realized how bad the storm was. Maybe it would be a good idea to change item number three. She could place the gift some-where else. Sarah had put her gift to the Piskies under a rhododendron bush in her own garden. She had a bush just like it, but Jimmy had said he hadn't seen the Piskies and he didn't think Sarah's wish came true. Even though Piskies were supposed to be all over Cornwall, nobody knew where they actually lived. Granny was the only person she knew who had seen them. Granny had seen them by Logan Rock.

A gust of wind thrust her forward into a stone hedge in the next field. It almost knocked her down. Peggy hoped she had not broken her grandmother's china saucer.

She switched on her torch. Her left hand was stinging. She had grazed her knuckles on the stones. Peggy sought shelter from the wind by crouching close to the hedge. It was stupid to go on in this storm. She should turn back while she had the chance, but where should she put her gift and make her wish? There was no question in her mind. She had to put her plan into motion tonight. If she didn't go all out tonight, she was absolutely sure that the evil horseshoe would win and her father would sell *The Sunrise*.

Sitting in her room and writing out her plans had been exciting. She had felt sure she had a chance, but the storm had changed everything. Peggy crouched closer to the hedge. The moment she stood up, the wind would grab her again.

It was getting late. The gift had to be given by eleven and she had a long way to go if she kept to her plan. She thought back to Granny's story about her great grandfather and how the Piskies had helped her to save him. She had said the Piskies she saw were the mystical beings of the Cornish coast, gifted with great powers. Granny didn't say just Cornish Piskies. Her plan had to work. It was her only hope. She had to make her wish to the Piskies who had great powers - the mystical beings of the Cornish coast. Peggy felt better now that she had made her decision. She stood up, bent her head to the wind, and struggled on.

On the open cliffs, the wind was a giant, invisible force. Peggy knelt down in the heather. The cliffs were different at night, alien and frightening. Thunder rolled, lightning flashed, the rain pelted down. There were other sounds, too - strange sounds that Peggy couldn't identify. Fervently she prayed that Granny Poldune was right about the Piskies not being bad souls. Souls were ghosts, weren't they? Those howling noises could mean that ghosts were on the cliffs with her!

Well, she couldn't think about that now. She had to stay on task. Shakily, Peggy got up and bent her body to the wind. She dropped to her knees often as she felt the wind pulling her towards the edge of the cliffs. The line of the cliff top was jagged and broken. There were several inlets; one wrong step, and she could step into space and fall onto the rocks, far below, rocks that the sea was pounding with white foamed fury.

Her torch beam was already weak. Peggy ran her tongue over her lips. She tasted salt. The wind had brought the sea to her. She moved to the right, further away from the edge, and without warning, she was flung onto her stomach into a gorse bush. She gasped in pain. Her face felt as though it had been slashed with razors. Then she felt a burning pain in her right ankle. Part of her boot was still caught inside a badger's hole. When Peggy pulled her foot out, her Wellington boot stayed inside the hole. She shone her torch on her ankle. It hurt when she moved it from side to side. She hoped she hadn't broken a bone. It began to throb.

With a sob, Peggy sat up and pulled her boot out of the badger's hole. There was water inside of it. She held it upside down and shook it. Carefully, she put it back on. Her ankle immediately protested the pressure of the boot. It probably was broken, she thought, her tears flowing faster. Her right cheek started to throb and sting. She tasted blood on her lips.

Peggy thrust her wet hand into the pocket of her mackintosh. The cream was still there. She tried the other pocket. The saucer seemed to be in one piece when she felt it through the dishtowel, but she stayed crouched amidst the heather, holding onto a scraggly bush.

Everything was going wrong. She couldn't get up and

fight the wind any more. It was too strong. She was afraid of falling over the cliff onto the rocks and into the angry sea. Besides, she reasoned, it was too late. Granny said she had to make the wish by eleven and it had to be past eleven now. "I can't," she whispered. "I can't do it!"

Peggy huddled into herself. She tucked her knees into her stomach and curled up into a ball. Her face stung, her ankle throbbed. It was too late, too hard. She had failed. Her plan had failed. Her body shook with sobs. She barely heard the thunder, did not see the lightning that lit up the sky, nor felt the rain that pelted down.

The cry of a lone seagull pieced through the noise of the storm. Peggy raised her head. She heard the cry again. It sounded just like Nimbob when something had scared him. Nimbob was lost! He was out in the storm, just like she was, and he was just as frightened. He could even be hurt, just like she was. Peggy struggled with her feelings. Nimbob needed her. She was the only one who cared that he was out in the storm, all alone. She was the only one who could save her precious, dear little cat.

Peggy sat up, wincing as a sharp pain ran up her leg. Nimbob was lost because of what she had done. Bad luck was filling the cottage, destroying her family. She had to do something about it! She had a plan. Her plan could still work, couldn't it? Peggy crawled, fell onto her stomach, pushed herself up, and crawled on through the storm. Her mind had found its focus again: Logan Rock, the gift, and to find Nimbob.

Chapter Twelve

Just One Wish

Logan Rock loomed above her. She was beginning to think that she would never, ever get there. The tears that ran down her face now were tears of relief. The giant rock sheltered her from the storm as she knelt down in the stubbly grass and felt for a smooth, flat place. She needed a safe place, a place sheltered from the winds and the rain. Peggy put her hand in her pocket and carefully removed the china saucer. She propped the torch on the granite ledge where she and Granny had sat. Its beam was even weaker now, but she had enough light to see. Peggy unwrapped the saucer. She stuffed the wet dishtowel back into her pocket. Peggy took the carton of cream and squeezed the sides until the thick cream plopped into the center of the saucer. Carefully, she placed it under the low granite ledge, replaced the lid, and slipped the wet cardboard carton back into her pocket.

Peggy coughed to clear her throat. She knelt beside the ledge and put her hand under it until she was touching the saucer.

"Piskies, Piskies, please hear me,
I bring a gift of cream for thee.
Accept the cream poured in this dish,
and please grant me just one wish"

She crouched for a while and listened. Granny had said that their voices were like silver bells, but she couldn't hear anything above the sounds of the storm that continued to rage on the cliffs.

Peggy retrieved her torch. She had to hurry back. She had to find Nimbob. Peggy moved back from the shelter of the huge rock. The wind grabbed her again, forcing her to drop to her knees. Gritting her teeth, Peggy began to retrace her steps.

Had the Piskies heard her over the noise of the storm?

Were they even there on a night such as this?

Granny had said they could read people's minds. Peggy hoped that this was true. The wind may have carried her spoken words out to sea.

Facing the terrors that had plagued her on her journey to Logan Rock, Peggy made slow progress on her return. She had paused on several occasions, unsure in the darkness of the way she knew so well. When the lightning flashed, giving her a brief look at the terrain, she struggled on. She was relieved to find the path to the fields, but her relief was short lived. Her Wellingtons kept slipping and catching in the ruts. Her right ankle protested every step. The lightning was now her only light. Her torch batteries were dead. She had shaken her torch and got a brief beam on two occasions, but even shaking it wouldn't make it work any more.

When she climbed over the last gate, she started to call Nimbob again. Her fear for him helped her to ignore the pain she felt as she limped to the front door. She had hoped he had found his way home and was waiting for her to let him in. He wasn't there. She limped around to the back door. It was so dark. She opened the door and turned on the scullery light. The storm was finally abating. The wind had died down, the thunder a distant rumble.

Peggy went out in the backyard. "Nimbob," she called. "Where are you?" It was faint, but she heard it clearly - a cat's cry of distress.

Suddenly, Peggy knew where Nimbob was. Limping, half laughing, and half crying, Peggy hurried to the chicken wire pen where they had raised the baby rabbits, the pen that had housed Mr. Fox, and now had trapped Nimbob. Peggy released the catch and opened the cage door. Nimbob leaped into her arms. His fur was soaking wet and he was trembling. Peggy hugged him and kissed him several times on the top of his little wet head.

She carried him into the cottage and still holding him, limped upstairs to the bathroom. She wrapped him in a towel. Only his ears, eyes, and nose were visible as she gently dried his fur. Nimbob sprang from her arms and ran down the stairs. Peggy grinned as she limped after him. She had a special treat for Nimbob tonight.

In the bathroom, Peggy removed her wet clothes. The bathtub was filled with her mother's wash. She would love to lie in a tub of hot water. She was chilled to the bone. No matter, she thought. She couldn't take a hot bath anyway. Mum would hear the water running.

Peggy hung her mackintosh on a hook on the back of the door. Her ankle hurt when she pulled off her wet jeans. She looked at it in the light. When she compared it to her left ankle, it was definitely bigger. It was bad luck finding that badger hole.

Peggy looked into the mirror to examine the scratches on her face. It had been a very prickly gorse bush. It was hard to see them. Her face was covered in mud. Her wet hair hung limply around her shoulders. She soaked a flannel in warm water and carefully washed the mud off her face. Ouch, her face was really stinging now. She could see the scratches. There were small scratches all over, but there were two deep ones on her right cheek and they were bleeding. Ruefully, she looked at the knuckles on her left hand. The skin was missing on two of them. "You got me three times in a row," she whispered. "Bad luck horseshoe, you have to go!"

Dressed in a warm flannel nightgown, Peggy limped painfully back downstairs and into the scullery. She hunted in the cupboard beside the stove and found just what she was looking for. Peggy carried it up to the bedroom with her. When she opened her door, Nimbob ran passed her, leaped onto her bed, and began his own personal clean up. Peggy grinned at him and limped to her chest of drawers.

Yawning, she set her bedside clock alarm for six o'clock. She would only have three hours sleep, but she mustn't over-sleep. "Wish must be made by half past seven," she murmured. Peggy limped back into the bathroom and felt in the pocket of her wet jeans for her Piskie charm. Clutching it in her hand, she fell into bed beside Nimbob, pulled her pillow disguise out, and was asleep the moment her head touched the pillow.

Chapter Thirteen

Tor

Sunbeams played upon Peggy's sleeping face. All signs of the storm were gone and the sky was a bright blue. "I see Nimbob came home safe and sound," said her father in his deep voice, awakening her. Peggy sat up. Her bedroom door was open. What time was it? In horror, she saw that it was six forty-five! The alarm had not gone off at six as it was supposed to.

She jumped out of bed and cried out in pain as her feet hit the floor. She had forgotten all about her ankle. Peggy sat back down on the bed to examine it. It was red and swollen. She limped into the bathroom. The wet clothes were not in the bathtub any more. Her mother was already working on them. There was no time for a shower, although she desperately needed one. Briefly she looked at her face. The deep scratches looked red and angry. She would have to spray that antiseptic stuff on them, but there was no time now. Peggy tried to brush her hair. Mud flakes fell into the basin. Yuck, her hair was such a mess.

Peggy limped back into the bedroom. Her clean, dry jeans were floods, but they had a flared bottom that helped when she pulled them over her bad ankle. She grabbed her last clean jumper from the drawer. It was white with pink flowers. She had planned to look her best when she made her wish, but this was the best that she could do.

Her mackintosh and Wellingtons were not in the bathroom where she had left them last night. She couldn't wear the raincoat. It would still be soaking wet, but she had to wear the Wellingtons. Peggy went back into the bedroom to get her jacket. She had been wearing it when her mother had ordered her to go to her room. Now she needed to get her boots without her parents seeing her, and she had to sneak out of the cottage.

Peggy went downstairs, doing her best to hide her limp. She hung her jacket on its usual peg by the front door. "Why aren't you fishing?" she asked her father, who usually left the cottage at five when he went to sea.

"I had to come back in. The storm did terrible damage to the pots last night. I lost some of 'em." Her father sipped his cup of hot tea.

"Will you be going out again?" Peggy asked anxiously.

"I have to put out some new pots and I'll be casting a line or two. You never know when the fish might bite."

Peggy sighed with relief. Dad had to go to sea today of all days. If the Piskies granted her wish, today would be his best day ever.

She looked at the kitchen clock. It was almost seven. She had to go!

"You went out after that cat, Peggy, after I told you not to," her mother said crossly, coming in from the scullery and holding up Peggy's mackintosh. "And there's a pile of wet, muddy clothes stuffed into the hamper for me to wash, not to mention your muddy tracks, and that cat's, all over my clean floors!"

Peggy, relieved that her mother had not guessed the

truth, was quick to apologize. She avoided looking at her mother so that she would not see the scratches on her face. "Sorry, Mum, I was so worried about Nimbob. Do you know where he was? He was ..."

"When I say you are not to go out and to stay in your room, I mean it, Peggy. Since you can't be trusted, you'll have to be watched. What I've done to have a daughter like you I'll never know." Her mother sniffed in disgust and went back into the scullery.

Peggy felt the sting of her mother's words, but she couldn't stop watching the kitchen clock. It was seven o'clock! Only thirty minutes to get back to Logan Rock and her father sat there at the kitchen table, drinking tea!

Her father got up from the table, yawned, stretched, and said, "Think I'll go down and get them extra pots from the fishing shed."

"Good idea, Dad," Peggy answered. Her father kept his pots and other fishing gear in a shed down on the stone plot where he parked his van. It was in the opposite direction to the cliffs. She watched her father put on his heavy sea jacket and wondered why he had suddenly become the slowest man on earth. He ambled into the kitchen to have a word with her mother. Hurry, Dad, she urged silently.

Peggy looked down at her stocking feet. Her Wellingtons must be in the scullery. Both her mother and her father were in the scullery so she couldn't get them. Quickly, she limped back upstairs and put on her trainers. The right shoe was too tight and it pressed on her sore ankle. "Ouch, that hurts!" she gasped. Peggy untied the laces and pulled out the flap. She limped to her chest of drawers, opened the top drawer, and took out the large piece of tin foil she had taken from the kitchen cupboard the night before.

Peggy peered over the banister to make sure her mother had not come into the kitchen and that her father had left. Peggy limped painfully, but as fast as she could, down the stairs. She put on her jacket. Her mother was running water in the scullery sink. Peggy looked at the kitchen clock. It was five minutes past seven. She groaned. Time was racing by. She hesitated at the front door. She looked up.

It had to be done. Peggy reached up and pried Tregarth's Good Luck horseshoe from its nails.

She still had one more stop to make. She limped down the path to the flower shed where her mother kept the picked daffodils in buckets of water. There were only empty buckets in the shed today. Inside the door, hanging on the wall, was just what she needed - a spade with a long handle. Peggy took the spade and closed the shed door.

The heifer field was a vast mud puddle. Peggy wished she had been able to get her Wellingtons. The mud oozed in her trainers and socks as she trudged through the field. The spade helped her to walk on her sore ankle. She used it like a walking stick and was able to hobble faster. She had wanted to put the horseshoe inside her jacket to free her other hand, but she was too afraid to place it next to her heart.

As quickly as she could, Peggy crossed the fields and came out onto the cliffs. They looked like her beautiful cliffs today, a far cry from the dark and alien cliffs of the night before. She wondered what time it was. It must be close to the deadline. She hurried on, her face twisted with pain.

An anxiety had been lurking in the back of her mind ever since she had first formulated her plan. She had not dared to address it. She had not even written it down. Her worry had now surfaced and demanded to be heard. How would the Piskies judge her? Peggy felt that queasy feeling in her stomach again. Granny had said that the Piskies judged people and if they found them lacking, they would not grant wishes. Would the Piskies find her lacking? Her mother definitely would. Peggy stumbled over some loose rocks and turned her sore ankle. "Ouch," she cried. Peggy gritted her teeth and hurried on. Time was running out. It must be past seven thirty. It was probably too late.

Logan Rock glinted in the bright morning sunshine as though it was set with a million tiny diamonds. Peggy stopped short. She was afraid to find her grandmother's bone china saucer - afraid of what the Piskies' answer would be. Peggy put the spade down, along with the horseshoe. Hesitant, she limped the last few steps to the granite ledge. She drew a deep breath, knelt down, and removed the china saucer.

The cream was gone. The center of the saucer glowed with a golden light. Peggy stood up and stared at the saucer in awe. The granite ledge, too, glowed. Glistening and shimmering in front of it was a golden circle. "The Piskies' magic circle," she whispered. She was actually standing in the Piskies' magic circle.

As Peggy was about to chant her rhyme, something moved above her. She looked up, and saw, with delight, the baby rabbits she and her mother had raised, hopping out of the chicken wire pen, and scampering into the fields.

The rabbits morphed into large gray and white sea gulls, their wings still stained, but free from oil, flying into the sky. They flew higher and higher, except for one, that became a baby magpie that grew up before her eyes and became a mother bird, nesting on her eggs.

In delight, Peggy saw the fox lying in the stone lane, leading to Chyoak. Farm dogs were racing across the road, and back across the fields to the sound of a whistle. She saw the fox run from the pen into the fields, passing several hedgehogs along the side of the primrose-covered hedgerows.

Peggy was mesmerized by the images. She felt fragile, light hands, hands as light as air on her shoulders, turning her around and around. Three times she was spun in a circle within the magic circle. Unbidden, her constant dream wish came into her mind: Tor, colored like the sands of Pedneyvounder, with a mane like the white foam of a stormy sea. The moment she thought of him, she saw him, galloping across the cliffs towards her, his mane flying in the wind. He was all she had ever dreamed of, and more. Silvery, sweet voices filled the air:

> *"Wish for him, Pegeen, Pegeen.*
> *Wish for him, Pegeen, Pegeen."*

Tor was closer now. She could see his nostrils flare and his creamy back gleam and ripple in the sun. Peggy gasped. Tor was wonderful! Peggy was floating amidst thousands of golden lights. She was gazing at Tor in total delight. She felt her feet touch the ground. There was an odd clunking sound. She saw Tregarth's Good Luck horseshoe lying just inside of the cottage door, small golden stars dancing away on the kitchen floor; she saw a Scottish purse seiner casting its net, catching hundreds of shiny mackerel, and then she saw a field of daffodils. The daffodils were all withering on their stems. Peggy took a deep breath:

> *"I wish, I wish, I wish,*
> *luck for my father with the fish.*
> *To keep The Sunrise is my wish."*

There was then stillness so still that Peggy could feel it surround her like a soft blanket. A moment later she heard the gulls shrieking, fighting and squabbling over scraps, the sea pounding the rocks below, and the wind in the heather. She looked for Tor, but Tor had vanished into the far off mist. When Peggy looked down, the magic, shimmering circle faded and was gone. Stunned by the wonder of it all, Peggy sank down on the granite ledge. She could still feel the gentle touch of the Piskies, and hear their silvery voices.

Tor. She had actually seen Tor, her beautiful wild stallion, galloping across the cliffs just as she had always imagined him. But no one should ever own Tor. He should always be wild, free to roam in the magical world of the Piskies.

When Peggy finally got up from the ledge, she saw something shimmering in a circle of sea pinks. Intrigued, she limped over to see what it could be. There, lying amongst the pretty flowers was a shiny, silver horseshoe. Peggy knelt down, and picked it up. It was a shoe from Tor. She just knew it. This was truly amazing.

Granny's words came into her mind. "…a horseshoe found in dawn's early light, cast off by a wild horse …"

"Thank you," she cried. "Oh, thank you, Tor."

"Thank you, Piskies, thank you, thank you, thank you!"

Peggy was reluctant to put the horseshoe down, but she had one more thing to do. Item number six on her plan list. She had to wrap the old purple-bound horseshoe in silver paper and bury it where it could do no harm.

Where to bury the horseshoe had been a difficult choice. She was afraid that the bad luck would seep through the ground and harm anyone or anything close to its burial place. The tin foil would protect to a certain extent, but would it be enough? The Piskie charm was not powerful enough to stop the bad luck, but the mystical Piskies of the Cornish coast would make sure it would do no harm.

It would be hard to find a place soft enough to dig a hole. The cliffs were rocky and the ground hard. Peggy looked over the area carefully. There was a pool of water beside a smaller rock to the right of Logan. Peggy limped over to her spade, picked it up, and returned to the small pool. She tried pushing the spade into the pool of water and was surprised to find that there was no resistance. She pulled the mud from the pool with her spade until she had a small mound.

When she went back to pick up the old horseshoe, she found that she didn't fear it or hate it anymore. In fact, she felt sad. She remembered all the times her father had tapped it for luck and had come home triumphant with a huge catch. Her mother had tapped it every year when it was time to harvest the flower crop. Peggy had helped her to pick and bunch thousands of beautiful daffodils. When she had knocked it down, all the remaining luck had poured out onto the kitchen floor. Then she had kicked it. Bad luck had come, so much bad luck, but it wasn't the horseshoe's fault.

Peggy pulled the silver tin foil from her pocket and carefully wrapped the old horseshoe. She took it over to the hole she had made and gently put it in. "I'm sorry," she whispered. Peggy covered it with the mound of mud and looked about her for some small rocks to add to its burial place.

Chapter Fourteen

Trust

The sun was high in the sky as Peggy limped painfully across the heifer field towards Chyoak. She was still filled with the wonder of it all, but her stomach felt queasy again. Mum would be waiting for her and she had no defense to offer.

Peggy returned the spade to the flower shed. She tucked Tor's shoe under her armpit inside her jacket. With dread, she hobbled up the garden path. Her mother was sitting at the kitchen table when Peggy opened the front door. She looked up, but said nothing. Peggy stood in the doorway. The silence was like a wall between them.

Peggy put her weight on both feet, and cried out. She sat on the bottom step of the stairs, and eased off her trainers. Her mother stood over her, and gave a cry of exasperation. "What have you done to your new trainers? Look at them! They're covered in mud, and Lord knows what else!"

"Sorry, Mum," Peggy said, her face twisted with pain. She eased off her right muddy, wet sock. Her mother's eyes widened at the sight of her swollen ankle. She knelt down and took Peggy's foot in her hands. She turned it to the right and then to the left. Peggy winced, but did not cry out. "It's not broken," her mother said and stood up again. "What did you do to your face?" she asked.

"I fell into a gorse bush. I have to put some of that antiseptic stuff on it." Peggy looked away from her mother's cold eyes. "Can I go to the bathroom?"

"You can," her mother said. "When you come down, I want to see you in the sitting room."

Peggy went up the stairs on her bottom. The sitting room, Peggy thought, in dismay. That's where all the serious talks took place. Good things were always shared in the kitchen.

Carefully, Peggy removed Tor's horseshoe from inside her jacket. She placed it reverently against the wall on the top of her chest of drawers, facing upward. She took the china saucer from her pocket and laid it beside the horseshoe. Peggy gazed at them for a moment before going into the bathroom. After she had used the toilet and washed her hands, Peggy came down the stairs, step by step on her bottom.

Her mother was sitting on the sofa. Antiseptic spray, some gauze, antibiotic cream, and some plasters were neatly set out on the table in front of her. "Sit," she ordered.

Peggy sat beside her mother, who took care of the cuts, scratches, and scrapes on her face and on her knuckles. "There," her mother said, putting the top back on the tube of antibiotic cream. "Your ankle will have to be soaked in iced water. We'll soak it and then we'll wrap it."

The sofa felt comfortable. Peggy leaned her head back against the pillow and closed her eyes. "Thank you, Mum," she said gratefully.

Her mother left the room and returned with a bowl of iced water. "Put your foot in that, Peggy," she said. "It'll help to bring the swelling down." Peggy did as she was told.

The cold water felt wonderful on her throbbing ankle.

"I went to the cove to look for you when you went out this morning, Peggy," her mother said. "Maybe it's a good thing I didn't find you. I was as mad as a hornet. Of course, I went to Granny Poldune's cottage. I knocked on the door and when she opened it, I demanded to know where you were."

"Granny didn't know where I was," Peggy said, puzzled.

"That's what she told me. She wouldn't let me in, and said she had work to be busy on. Then she closed the door in my face."

Peggy grinned. "She always does that," she said.

"I was leaving the cove. I had looked for you all over, even though it was obvious that you weren't there. I was talking to myself, planning what I would do to you when I did get hold of you. Granny was on the path. She barred my way."

"What did she say, Mum?"

"At first I wouldn't listen to the old woman. I tried to get past her, but she held on to my arm. 'Peggy is a good girl,' she said. 'There are things afoot, Jean, about which you have no notion.'"

Peggy squirmed. She wanted to tell her mother about the horseshoe herself. "What did she tell you?" she asked.

"Well, Peggy, to tell you the truth I needed to hear some kind of explanation of your behavior. It was breaking my heart. I tried to pull my arm away from her, but she held fast. Then I stopped trying to get passed her. The fight just went out of me. I stood on the path in front of her, quiet."

Peggy nodded. "Granny likes that," she said.

"She didn't say anything for a minute or two and then she said, 'Peggy is doing her best to help you and yours in her own way. Trust is a terrible thing to misplace, Jean. If you misplace the trust in those you love, it is you who will be destroyed. I'll say no more.' And she wouldn't! No matter what I said to her, she wouldn't answer me. She went back over to her cottage, went in, and shut the door." Her mother looked at her, a hopeful expression on her face. "Now what do you have to say, Peggy?"

Peggy looked down at the green oval rug on the floor. "It's complicated, Mum," she said.

"Complicated, Peggy? Will you please tell me what is going on?"

"Granny is right, Mum. I am trying to help. I know I should have come to the daffodil fields and helped you with the wash, but things came up and I couldn't." Peggy looked at her mother, tears in her eyes.

"What things?" her mother asked in a quiet tone. "Trust is a two-way street in my book."

"I can tell you some things, Mum, but some things have to be a secret."

"Why?" her mother demanded, her tone sharper.

"First, I knocked down Tregarth's Good Luck, and then I kicked it."

Her mother's face flushed with anger. "Of all the careless, thoughtless ..."

"It was an accident, Mum. I slammed the door. You know you are always telling me not to slam the door, but I keep doing it and that's how I knocked Tregarth's Good Luck right off its nails. I put it back so you and Dad wouldn't know about it, but the good luck it used to give us was gone. Bad luck came instead. Nimbob got a splinter of china in his paw and you hurt your finger and Dad's fishing was bad and it kept up. Then we got eelworm in the daffs and ...."

Her mother put up a protesting hand to stop her. "You should have told us, Peggy, but good luck is when you try hard and everything goes well. It's the icing on the cake. Bad luck is when you try your best and things that should work, don't work at all. But what's this got to do with your disobedience? Every time I turned my back you took off like a jack rabbit, no matter what I had asked you to do."

"I had to fix it, Mum. I had to reverse the bad luck."

"What did you do?" her mother asked curiously.

Peggy sighed. "I'll take the punishment, Mum. I can't tell you. I'm sorry."

"Is Granny Poldune in on this with you?" her mother asked, an irritated note in her voice.

"I told Granny about the horseshoe. She said I had to bury it to stop the bad luck, but she wouldn't help me to reverse what I had done. She shut the door in my face just like she did to you." Peggy reached down and touched her ankle. "It still hurts," she said.

Her mother stared at Peggy in disbelief. "Did you say that Granny told you to bury your father's horseshoe? Tregarth's Good Luck horseshoe, hung on the door by your great grandfather? You didn't, did you?" She jumped up, and ran to the sitting room doorway. Her hand flew to her mouth. "It's gone!" she cried.

Peggy took her foot out of the bowl of water. She got up and limped painfully to the door. "Wait, Mum," she said. Peggy went back upstairs on her bottom, and limped into the bedroom. She picked up Tor's shoe, and came back downstairs, holding it carefully so that it would not turn upside down.

Her mother was still standing at the bottom of the stairs,

staring up at the space where Tregarth's Good Luck had once been. "I can't believe you did this, Peggy. Your father holds that horseshoe in his heart."

Peggy nodded. "I know, Mum. I was so upset when I knocked it down and everything went wrong, but look, Mum. This horseshoe will be the luckiest horseshoe in the whole world."

Her mother barely glanced at the shiny, silver horseshoe Peggy held up with pride. "You can't buy a horseshoe, Peggy, and expect it to be the same at all. I wondered why you were taking money out of your bank." She turned to look at Peggy, sitting on the bottom step of the stairs. "Where did you bury it? I'll go out right now before your father gets back, and get it."

Peggy shook her head. "Mum, it won't work any more. All the good luck fell out of it when I knocked it down, and left it on the kitchen floor. Granny is right. She said I had to bury it where it would do no harm."

"It's not the good luck I am concerned with, Peggy," her mother said. "I am far more concerned about your father."

"Mum, please, just hold it in your hand for a minute, please?" Peggy pleaded. She held the horseshoe out to her mother.

Reluctantly, her mother took the horseshoe. She looked at it, puzzled. "It's a real horseshoe," she said. "It feels real right enough, but it's silver. Where did you get this, Peggy?" She continued to stare at the beautiful horseshoe. "It sparkles like the sunlight on the water," she said, in awe.

"I know," Peggy said. "It's so lovely."

"Where did you get it?" her mother asked her again.

"That's a secret, Mum," Peggy answered. "I promise,

Mum, that this horseshoe is very, very lucky. Please believe me, Mum."

"That's the oddest thing. I do believe you, Peggy," her mother said. "It feels very special." She stroked the surface of the horseshoe gently with one finger.

"It is, Mum. It's very special. We have to cover it with wool, every inch of it, and hang it in one place," Peggy said, repeating Granny Poldune's words.

Her mother looked up at the back of the cottage door, straightened, and nodded. "Right," she said. She handed the horseshoe back to Peggy. "We'll have to hurry, Peg, before your father gets home." She ran into the sitting room, and rummaged in her bag of wools. Triumphant, she pulled out some purple wool. It wasn't the exact shade of the wool that had bound the other horseshoe. It was a lighter color, but she could work with it.

She ran passed Peggy into the scullery. "What are you doing, Mum?" Peggy cried.

"I'm going to soak this wool in some cold tea," her mother called back.

"But Mum, you'll get the wool all stained that way," Peggy protested.

"Hopefully it will look older, too," her mother said.

Peggy lay on the couch with her ankle bandaged, feeling much, much better. Her mother sat in her father's armchair. After they had bound Tor's shoe with the wet, tea-stained purple wool, covering every inch of it, they had hung it on the inside of the cottage door.

Her mother had made her some lunch and had given her two ibuprofen pills to help to bring the swelling down on her ankle, and to ease the pain. Peggy felt her eyes closing. "You know, Peg, I've been making mistakes, too," her mother said.

Peggy struggled to sit up. "What, Mum?"

"My mother, God rest her soul, told me everything. I don't think there was a single day when my mother didn't share her problems with me. I couldn't sleep at night for worrying about them." Her mother picked up a photograph of Peggy's grandmother from the side table beside the chair, and smiled at it. "She worried about everything and she made me worry about everything, too."

"Grandma did that?" Peggy asked. "What kind of problems, Mum?"

"Oh, that doesn't matter now, Peg," her mother said, smiling at her. "What I'm trying to say is that I didn't want to worry you like my mother worried me, but I was wrong. I should have pulled your head out of your school books and told you what was going on with our family. I put a distance between us by not sharing things with you. When you knocked down that horseshoe, you thought everything was your fault."

"It was!" Peggy said.

Her mother laughed. "The trawlers have been here for weeks, Peg, and the daffs have been dying for days, only I didn't know what was wrong with them. I believe in luck, Peggy, good and bad, and we have had nothing but bad luck for some time, but it wasn't all your fault."

Her mother got up and came over to her. "Granny was right, Peg. Trust is a terrible thing to misplace. I think we both misplaced our trust in each other." Peggy nodded. A lump was forming in her throat. Her mother was smiling down at her. Her eyes were gentle, kind eyes. "I only misplaced my trust for a while, Peg, and it's such a gift to find it again."

Peggy reached up as her mother bent down, and they hugged each other. "I love you, Mum," Peggy whispered.

Chapter Fifteen

Luck for the Tregarths

The cottage was quiet. Nimbob was curled up on Peggy's stomach as she lay sleeping on the couch. The front door burst open and her father came into the kitchen. "Good news, Jean," he cried.

Peggy sat up. Nimbob jumped off her lap. Her mother hurried out of the scullery. "What is it, Bill?" she asked.

"They've imposed a three mile limit on any boat over thirty-five feet, Jean, and what's more there's a quota on how much fish can be caught." Her father was grinning from ear to ear. "What do you think about that?"

"I love it," her mother exclaimed. "The trawlers can't cast their nets to our shores any more!"

Peggy hobbled to the sitting room door, still half asleep. "Dad, you are supposed to be out fishing! Today was supposed to be your luckiest day ever," she cried.

"It is, Peg, it is." He repeated what he had told her mother. "The news came over the radio early this morning."

He turned to her mother. "I wanted to get right back, and tell you all about it, Jean, but you know I had that business in town to take care of. Then I went to Brian Travis's flower farm, like we discussed."

"Well, get on with it," her mother said, smiling.

Her father turned to Peggy. "Excuse us, Peggy."

Disappointed, Peggy turned back into the sitting room and was about to shut the door when her mother said, "Come on to the kitchen table, Peg. We'll have a nice cup of tea and hear the news together."

"I want to tell you about the loan," her father said to her mother.

"I know that, Bill, but it's time to include our Peg, don't you think?"

Her father looked surprised for a moment, nodded, and said, "Whatever you think is best, Jean."

As Peggy limped over to the table, her father said, "You're in the wars. What happened to you? Scratched your face and all."

"I fell in a badger hole, Dad," Peggy said with a grin.

"See what you get?" Her father pulled out a kitchen chair for her to sit on. "You are always off helping the wild and this is what you get for your troubles."

Peggy laughed. She felt a bubble of joy explode inside her. Her reward for helping the wild was unbelievably wonderful. It was how the Piskies had judged her and that's why they had heard her wish. "It's okay, Dad," she managed to say.

There was a sharp rap at the cottage door. Her father went to answer it. "I'd like to take a look at your boat now," a man's voice said.

"Sorry, Mr. Tyler," her father said. "There's been a change in plans. *The Sunrise* is no longer for sale."

"But I came all the way out here," Mr. Tyler protested.

"Sorry for your trouble. Good evening to you." Her father closed the door.

Peggy and her mother exchanged a relieved glance, but

said nothing. "Now," her father said, coming back to the kitchen table. "Where was I? Good news, all good news!"

Her father had arranged a small loan from the bank to tide them over and it was the breaking news that the trawlers could no longer fish the coastal waters that had helped the loan to go through.

Her mother was very pleased to hear that Brian Travis had said that she could harvest all the violet runners she could use in exchange for some fresh fish and a crab or two. She knew that the runners were available in April, but she wasn't sure she could get them. Happily her mother planned her next crop – violets in the daffodil fields. She could start picking them in September and the Christmas market would be especially good. Peggy eagerly offered to help to dig up all the daffodil bulbs, destroy them, and to help plant the violet runners. It was an offer her mother was pleased to accept. Her father also wanted to help to clear the fields. With the three of them working together, it would be a family making light work.

They sat at the kitchen table, sipping hot tea and eating scones that her mother had baked while Peggy was asleep. The news was all good. Peggy felt happy. But what was making her feel especially happy was that she was at the table, with her parents, and for the first time in a very long time, she felt a part of them, a part of the family.

As her mother cleared up, everybody was talking at once, busy with plans, eager for the changes in their lives. Bill Tregarth walked over to the front door. "Three times lucky! You're a good friend," he said, and reached up to tap Tregarth's Good Luck.

Peggy froze in mid-sentence. Her mother stood in the scullery doorway like a statue. Bill Tregarth looked at his fingers. "It's wet," he exclaimed. He rubbed his fingers against each other. "You should be more careful, Peg, letting the storm in like you did. There was water and mud all over the house, and you've got our lucky horseshoe all wet."

"Sorry, Dad," Peggy said.

She would tell him all about it one day. There would come a time when it would be right to tell him, but that time was not today.

Chapter Sixteen

Lovely Day

The Parish Church was packed to an overflow the following Sunday. The vicar's sermon was strong with faith being his main theme. He had carried a heavy burden over the past few months and was at a loss how to help many of his parishioners. It may take a while, but there was cause for celebration and he took full advantage of it.

Peggy's ankle was much better and she could walk quite well with the aid of the walking stick her father had made for her from a blackthorn bush. The scratches on her face were healing, as were the scrapes on her knuckles. The previous Wednesday, when the scratches had become infected, her mother had made Granny Poldune a Cornish pasty and had taken it down to her. She had returned with a small jar of ointment that Peggy had to apply to the scratches on her face and scrapes on her knuckles two nights in a row. The cream was dark green, thick, and smelled very strange, but Peggy had applied it without question. She had even tried it on the pimples on her forehead.

Jimmy Wallace waved to her from his back seat in the choir. Peggy waved back.

After the service, people gathered outside. Trevor Vernon was telling everybody who would listen that he had decked a Scot in the local pub. Since he had a black eye, Peggy wondered who had really been decked, Mr. Vernon or the Scot.

A tall girl with blond curly hair was standing beside Mrs. Wallace. They were chatting with Mr. and Mrs. Rogers. That must be Sarah, she thought, and wondered if Jimmy would tell her that he had let the cats out and that they had eaten the clotted cream she had intended as a gift for the Piskies.

Later that afternoon, there was a knock on the cottage door. It was Jimmy. Her mother invited him in and told Peggy they could talk in the sitting room. Peggy grabbed her walking stick and said they would go down to the cove. She wanted to show Jimmy *The Sunrise.*

Once outside, Jimmy eagerly asked Peggy if she had asked her father about going out in the boat to look for hidden caves. Excited, Peggy told him that her father had said he would take them both out the following Sunday.

"Sarah said I had to come right back and tell her what you said about the Piskies," Jimmy said.

"Piskies? What Piskies?" Peggy said with a grin.

Jimmy laughed. "It's like making a wish on a birthday cake. If you blow all the candles out, you can make a wish. If you tell anybody the wish, it won't come true."

Peggy nodded. "Something like that," she agreed.

"Well, I've made the same wish every year since I was ten, and I've never told a soul, and it still hasn't come true."

"What is it?" asked Peggy curiously.

"Can't tell you. It won't come true," he said. They both burst into laughter.

"I told Sarah," Jimmy said.

"Was she mad at you?" Peggy asked.

"My sister is a wildcat! She was furious that I hadn't

told her before, and she grabbed one of the sofa cushions and threw it at me." Jimmy grinned. "She missed because I ducked and the cushion knocked over one of Mum's best lamps. Mum was fit to be tied about her lamp, so I told Mum I had done it. Sarah said I was a liar, always was, and always would be a liar, and that she had done it."

Peggy laughed. "Is she still mad?"

"No, I don't think so," Jimmy said. "She brought some bloke she met at University home for Easter."

"Do you like him?" Peggy asked.

Jimmy shrugged. "He plays football," he said.

When Peggy saw a hedgehog lying on its back by the side of the hedgerow, she knelt down and gently flipped it over. Immediately the hedgehog became a spiky ball.

They stopped at the entrance to the cove, beside the running stream. "What's that?" Jimmy asked, pointing to a huge green plant with spiky stalks and broad leaves.

"It's a Gunnera," Peggy said.

"I didn't pass Tramp's class. I couldn't remember all the names of the plants."

"I love Mr. Tramper's class," Peggy said excitedly. "He showed us a film about whales. They were incredible!"

"Oh, yes, I remember that," Jimmy said. "What do you think of Lynch?" Animatedly, Peggy and Jimmy discussed their school and teachers as they walked into the cove.

The cove was peaceful. The same old man that Peggy had seen on the day she had come to the cove to seek Granny Poldune's help, was sitting on the bench and soaking up the sun. "Lovely day," he said as they passed him.

"Lovely day," Peggy agreed, this time looking at him, and smiling.

Granny Poldune was gathering seaweed on the rocks.

Peggy watched her for a moment and felt both gratitude and affection well up inside her. Granny had known all along what to do and had told her in her own way. She was just too thick to see it at the time. Peggy waved to her. Granny waved back and came over the rocks towards them.

"That old woman is coming over here!" Jimmy said. "Sarah says she's a witch."

Peggy smiled and limped towards Granny Poldune. "Got something for you, Peggy," Granny Poldune said. She put her hand into her cardigan pocket and pulled out Peggy's watch.

Peggy was delighted. "Thank you," she said. "Where did you find it?"

Granny Poldune waved her hand into the air. "Found it here and there," she said. "You had no need of it. There is no such thing as time in the world of those we know, but will not speak about."

Peggy nodded her understanding. "Thank you, Granny." She put the watch back on her wrist and buckled it.

Granny Poldune looked into Peggy's eyes for a long moment. Pride for the girl who stood before her shone in her wise, gray eyes. She hung her bag of seaweed over her arm and crossed the slip to go to her cottage.

Jimmy watched her go. "What was that all about?" he asked. "You know that old woman? Sarah may be right, you know. She looks like a witch to me."

Peggy limped over to her father's boat. "Here's *The Sunrise*," she said.

"Brilliant," Jimmy said, as he admired her father's boat. "I can't wait until next Sunday." Jimmy climbed into the boat chatting to her about the caves he was convinced they would find and one day would explore.

Peggy was looking over at Granny Poldune's cottage. Smoke spiraled from the chimney. Peggy thought about what Jimmy had said about her. Maybe she was a witch. She had never really thought about it. Granny was – well, she was Granny Poldune. Peggy sat on the edge of the boat, and swung her legs carefully over and into it. It really didn't matter one way or the other, but if Granny Poldune was a witch, she was the best witch in the whole world!

Glossary of English Words

Biscuit	Cookie
Bloke	Guy
Cardigan	Open sweater with buttons
Chap	Man
Chemist	Pharmacy
Cornish Pasty	Pastry filled with meat, potatoes, and vegetables
Crisps	Potato chips
Flannel	Washcloth
Hairdressers	Beauty Shop
Holidays	Vacation
Humbug	Candy
Jar	Pot
Jumper	Sweater
Larder	Pantry
Mackintosh	Gabardine raincoat
Pigtails	Braids
Pinch	Steal
Plaster	Band Aid
Porridge	Oatmeal
Purse Seiner	Fishing trawler
Rubbish	Trash
Scullery	Room adjacent to kitchen, used to prepare and store food
Shop	Store
Spade	Shovel
Sweets	Candy
Tea	Light meal, served late afternoon
Telly	Television
Tinfoil	Aluminum Foil
Torch	Flashlight
Trainers	Sneakers
Vicar	Priest, pastor
Wardrobe	Closet
Wellingtons	Rubber boots

3343404

Made in the USA